W9-BPL-283

the old ballerina

the old
BALLERINA

ELLEN COONEY

COFFEE HOUSE PRESS

MINNEAPOLIS

NOV 0 4 1999
OAK LAWN LIBRARY

COPYRIGHT © 1999 by Ellen Cooney
BOOK & JACKET DESIGN by Kelly Kofron
COVER PHOTOGRAPH © by Nicholas De Vore / *Tony Stone Images*
AUTHOR PHOTOGRAPH by Debi Milligan

Coffee House Press is an independent nonprofit literary press
supported in part by a grant provided by the Minnesota State Arts Board,
through an appropriation by the Minnesota State Legislature,
and in part by a grant from the National Endowment for the Arts.
Significant support has also been provided by the McKnight Foundation;
Lannan Foundation; the Lila Wallace Reader's Digest Fund;
Jerome Foundation; Target Stores, Dayton's, and Mervyn's by the Dayton
Hudson Foundation; General Mills Foundation; St. Paul Companies;
Butler Family Foundation; Honeywell Foundation; Star Tribune Foundation;
James R. Thorpe Foundation; Dain Bosworth Foundation; Pentair, Inc.;
the Helen L. Kuehn Fund of the Minneapolis Foundation; the law firm of
Schwegman, Lundberg, Woessner & Kluth, P.A.; and many individual donors.
To you and our many readers across the country,
we send our thanks for your continuing support.

Coffee House Press books are available to the trade through our primary
distributor, Consortium Book Sales & Distribution, 1045 Westgate Drive,
Saint Paul, MN 55114. For personal orders, catalogs, or other information,
write to: Coffee House Press, 27 North Fourth Street, Suite 400,
Minneapolis, MN 55401.

Good books are brewing at coffeehousepress.org

LIBRARY OF CONGRESS CIP INFORMATION
Cooney, Ellen.
The old ballerina: a novel/Ellen Cooney.
p.   cm.
ISBN 1-56689-086-1 (alk. paper)
I. Title.
PS3553.05788 043   1999
813'.54—dc21
99-35462   CIP

10   9   8   7   6   5   4   3   2   1

to Cynthia Ozick

———————————————

contents

margaret

lisette

class

nibora

mr. friedrich

a stolen room

a white hole

sissy

marybeth

billy

a meeting

doreen

shaun

inside

boy one

davey

class

the hazeltons

mr. bird

class

the silver monkey

margaret

MY LIFE AS a health care aide imposter began accidentally on a clear bright morning in April, at the Nashway Valley Home Health Care Associates on lower Main Street, in a gray and derelict part of town.

The woman who cleaned the Nashway was my neighbor: she lived in my building, across the hall. She was seventy or seventy-five, and her ankles were always swollen, the skin spilling over the sides of her dirty white sneakers, which never had laces in the eyelets. She was older than me by twenty years but I preferred to think of it as two hundred. She looked like an old-fashioned gypsy fortune-teller—in fact, she was Greek, from a family that used to run a pizza shop downtown, which had closed many years ago, when Papa Gino's moved into the mall. Her name was Panadopolous, Mrs. Dee Panadopolous. The Dee was a shortening of an unpronounceable name with many vowels. It did not seem right to me that she should be cleaning an office building at her age, with those feet.

And she had hairs on her chin, gray hairs. An old woman's dark moustache ran the length of her upper lip, without touching the lip itself, as if she'd been drinking a chocolate frappe.

"I have used up my sick days. My stomach and heart are not well. Will you go in my place tomorrow morning to the office I clean?"

I'd never done cleaning before on a professional level, but what was to learn? Grime was grime. You rolled up your sleeves and got rid of it.

We had talked at the door of my apartment. My neighbor felt too weak to do anything more than trudge across our hallway to ask her question, press a key in my hand, and say, "Be sure to go early in the morning. When I get my next paycheck I will give you twenty dollars."

I'd been laid off my job in the shipping department of the plastics factory by the river, where I worked for eighteen years. In the last four months, I could find no work at all, not even a few odd hours here and there of baby-sitting, or one tiny glimmer of hope from the forms I filled out every week downtown at the unemployment office, or the applications I kept pressing, without despair, into the hands of clerks in personnel offices at our town's three other factories. The shipping operations in these places were done by computer. All the people being hired to work at the computers were young.

It was the pinching of pennies that bothered and hurt me the most. I felt pinched, like a foot being squeezed into a shoe that was three or four sizes too small.

WHEN I WALK into the Nashway office, a phone is ringing, but it's answered by machine, with the sound off.

I sit down at a desk. I look at a few brochures describing Nashway services. I light a cigarette, smoke it. There are ashtrays, which you would not expect to find in the office of health care people. I wave at the air where the smoke curls thickly in streamers of sunlight. I feel like Goldilocks. I spit on a piece of kleenex and put the used-up cigarette into it, and the ashes, too. With another bit of tissue I wipe the ashtray clean.

"Today I'm the cleaning lady," I say to the desks and the chairs.

After several minutes of looking through drawers, I begin to feel at home. I would have set about at once with the business of cleaning, but I hadn't discovered a storage area for buckets, rags, ammonia, scouring powder, Windex, brooms, mops, a vacuum cleaner, rubber gloves. It was possible that

Mrs. Panadopolous brought these things herself, and had forgotten to mention this part of it. I can't recall a single time I noticed my old neighbor going out from the building at all, never mind carrying objects, although of course she must have done so.

I'm just about ready to call up my neighbor on the phone and ask her what to do, when a little red sportscar comes into the yard. It enters through the old front gates. If small foreign sportscars can have feelings, this one looked nervous —and no wonder. It's strange and unbelievable that a company of health care professionals had chosen this kind of place for their office.

The Nashway building used to be the headquarters of a school transportation company called Haemer's Orange Coaches: seven or eight years ago, it went bankrupt. Before that, it was the showroom of a car dealership, which had undergone the same fate. There is a large, cluttered room inside, surrounded by plate glass windows. Perhaps the people from Haemer's intended to return some day and collect the remains of their fleet, if "fleet" was what they called it.

It looked as if they'd left in a hurry. Dark orange buses, station wagons, and vans stand every which way, at strange angles, slowly being eaten by rust. New spring grasses poke up around their axles. Steering wheels are missing. Doors are off hinges. Places where seats had been removed look like missing teeth in an open, grinning mouth. Some of the vehicles are up on cinder blocks, and some are up on jacks. A few are tipped over on their sides, as if the hand of a giant had pushed them. A few are intact, and look dignified and solemn, like worn-out creatures who stopped in their tracks a long time ago, and made up their minds to be fossils.

The sunlight on that rust is the color of mustard mixed with honey. Here and there, in brief, silver sparks, the early morning light shines like crazy off engine parts and loose bits of chrome. Rearview mirrors that had fallen face-up in the dirt are as shiny and loose in this light as puddles of mercury. Mrs. Panadopolous must have cared about the windows of the office: they are spotless, as if the glass were empty air. The windows are the only things here that are clean, in a way that you would notice.

I look out the big windows and do not feel alarmed, although I probably should have.

Getting out of the car is an odd-looking man in a wrinkled but expensive tan raincoat, buttoned all the way up, as if protecting his throat from a chill. The man is heavy-boned and tall in a startling way—not bulky or awkward, just large.

The odd-looking man looks slowly and calmly around the yard, taking everything in without being alarmed, without judgement. It's obvious that he's never been here before.

He appears at my side so quickly—I jump a little—I have the sense he must have entered the office in one step, quick and silent like a ghost, as if straight through the door, without opening it.

In spite of his size he walks lightly. If he carried a large bowl of water, filled to the brim, not a drop of it would have spilled; it would not have even rippled. But he doesn't seem rich. "Rich" is not what I think of. He looks at me directly when he speaks to me, and he doesn't seem false and affected, or smooth on the outside but brittle underneath, as you expect in someone wealthy, like a seashell lacquered over with varnish.

He tells me his name immediately. "I am so-and-so," he says. It sounds like "brrr," as if he is trying to tell me that in spite of the beautiful day, he is freezing; and his voice is low and mumbly, so I wonder if he suffers from a toothache. I act as if I'd heard him perfectly well. Mr. Brrr.

Mr. Brrr is almost totally bald. His big head is so exposed, like the skin on top of a mushroom, I want to say to him, "Put a hat on." It's uncomfortable to be seeing someone's skull like this, as if you stumbled on a secret that maybe you shouldn't have looked at, but then you can't look anywhere else.

He has a stoop in his shoulders. Oh, he's a hunchback, you'd think, except that the hunching is evenly distributed.

His face is pale, like a man who rarely sees sunlight. I guess his age to be close to my own, but he could have been many years older. His eyes are dark, and deeply set in. His cheekbones are very large and the top of his face protrudes outward, in a jutting, angular way, like a Neanderthal in a history book. But it seems that this is something Mr. Brrr must have known about himself. The element of fright, upon meeting him, only lasts for a couple of seconds.

"Mrs. Eberhart?"

I know from the brochures that Evelyn Eberhart is the name of the manager of the Nashway. I answer without lying. "Oh, she'll be sorry when she finds out she missed you."

"I have so little time. I'm afraid I hadn't left her with a way to contact me. I should have been here yesterday. You are, perhaps, the available aide, whom she had mentioned to me on the phone?"

Mr. Brrr takes an envelope from a pocket of the raincoat. Tilting my head forward, just a little, I give the impression that I am nodding.

"I apologize for asking you to handle this account. I didn't mean to be unorthodox, when Mrs. Eberhart had made it clear to me that arrangements must be made through only her. I was worried I might have bungled all this, when I had thought it would be so simple. I'd tried three other agencies already, without success."

"You've hit it on the head just fine right now, I would say."

He waves the envelope in the air. "Mrs. Eberhart had mentioned a form I'd fill out, but I'm hoping you'll take care of that end. The information you'll need is in here. The suggested amount of time you'll be employed is two months. I expect, though, that two months may not be enough, in which case, I'm quite certain, I'll be notified. But let's say for now that we'll cross that particular bridge when someone builds it."

"You're not the patient?"

"No, I am not, but I can see where you would think so. I am a teacher in the high school. I believe I had made it clear to Mrs. Eberhart that my friend is a woman."

"This information, it's the only copy?"

"Oh, yes. The woman whose account I'm setting up, I must tell you, although I clearly made this point to Mrs. Eberhart, is very private, and to tell you the truth, I don't blame her."

"You don't look like a teacher, if you don't mind my saying so," I tell him, because I'd had the impression that this fact about himself was something he had invented, spontaneously, for some reason. He nods his head and says, in a gentle voice, "Thank you for the compliment. My friend says I look like Aeneas of Troy, that is, the Aeneas of after the war, before he founded Rome."

"I was never that good in school."

"Aeneas had a hard time of it," he says, and I ask him, "How sick is your friend?"

"She's had a hip operation," he says. "I believe I pointed that out to Mrs. Eberhart."

"Oh, she was vague when it came to particulars."

"I wonder, would it be out of the question to ask you to go and meet my friend quite soon? She's not well, you see."

"I can go today. This woman, she's not your wife?"

Mr. Brrr isn't wearing a wedding ring, but I felt like asking anyway.

His eyes open wide. "My wife? Oh, my. Oh, no. Oh, my goodness."

"Hey. I only mentioned it because, I needed to know."

My voice sounds rougher—my whole manner is rougher—than I intended. But anyone else who has ever had a stroke of good luck for a change, just suddenly out of nowhere one day, would understand how I felt at this moment. If a feather had touched my cheek, I would gear myself up for the brick that would come the next moment, having loosened itself from a wall somewhere: it would fall on top of my head.

But Mr. Brrr sees nothing of my distress. He says, "Marriage is something which my friend had thought of trying several times, without ever quite managing to make a go of it."

"Then I guess we'll have something in common," I tell him, and he smiles at me sadly, like a softening in his mask of formality. "Don't tell me anything personal, because, even if I had the time to stand here and talk with you more, I wouldn't be able to bear it," is what he really seems to be saying.

My pleasure in his company is brief, and disappears as quickly as that soft, sad smile of his.

He holds out the envelope and I accept it. He hurries away, and my fears intensify. If he comes back in, saying, "I've changed my mind," or, "There's been a terrible mistake," what could I do? He would reach for the envelope. He would try to grab it away from me. Would we tear it in half? No, wait—the bottoms of his shoes would be caked with dirt from the yard. He might have slipped. If he fell to the floor, his huge head would strike a desk leg; he'd be concussed. Lying there bleeding, he would expect me to know, and to offer him, the appropriate type of first aid.

But the red car pulls away, looking shiny and vigorous. It never before in its life felt as relieved as it did then, to get away from the hulks of the buses. It slides into the street, turns the corner by two old warehouses, and vanishes. I open the envelope. There's a single page of notepaper inside, as thin and crisp as a paint chip.

"My name is Irene Kamsky," it says.

The style of the writing is narrow and spikey. Mrs. Kamsky had formed letters that looked a little bit taller than they needed to be; all the words were spaced a little too widely apart. It looks as if Mrs. Kamsky had written with a needle dipped in ink. When I turn the paper over, the ink does not show through, not at all.

Mrs. Irene Kamsky is fifty-eight years old. She lives alone in a suburb north of town. She suffers from a debilitative form of arthritis, and recently had surgery for a hip replacement.

I know of the suburb although I'd never been there. "Well-off" is how I've always heard it described.

The note says, "As my friend must have made you aware, I wish to have a health care aide, or personal attendant, as you are sometimes also called, of experience, who is quiet and discreet, who respects a person's privacy, and who is tolerant of demands put upon you that may be slightly different from demands put upon you in the past. Willingness to act as driver to me on occasions when I am unable to do so will be welcomed. Having your own car is not necessary. I will pay you in cash, on a regular monthly schedule."

It's been a while since I had a valid driver's license. When you're unemployed you tend to let things lapse. But I say to myself, "Margaret, don't be picky."

PROBABLY, from the point of view of a health care aide, the best time of all, in terms of one's patient, would be the time when you haven't yet met, when you are free to invent, from a small set of facts on one piece of paper, a whole person, who was reasonable, well-groomed, and good-natured, and who did not chatter aimlessly, or whine and complain, or make demands every minute for the sake of just making demands; and they would never take out their bad moods on you, or feel bitter and hard, in spite of whatever was wrong with them, which had caused them to need you in the first place.

In their earliest forms, patients of health care aides must seem like friendly, well-meaning phantoms. You hold in your hand a sheet of paper: looking up from it, you stare into the future optimistically, and picture the new person as if their single purpose in life was to quietly wait for you, as harmless as a pillar of fog, on a comfortable sofa in a comfortable room. If things take place to disappoint you, or when you feel disappointment most deeply, you can always look back to those airy, light beginnings, and remember how fond of the patient you had been, even though it was brief, and even though, to begin with, it was only just illusions.

So if things turned out to be awful, really awful, I could look at Mrs. Kamsky and say, "When I first began to think about you, you were a blob to me, a white blob, and I liked you that way a lot better."

WHEN I SEE where she lives, an old familiar feeling comes over me, of my hopes closing up, as the fingers of a hand make a fist.

Her house is only a simple, ordinary ranch, with gray shingles. It is low to the ground, and absolutely, in every pore of its being, without character. In shape, by the way it presents itself to the road, it looks like a gray cigar box on which someone had placed a roof; that's about how small it looks, too. And those shingles make it worse. Those shingles! They make it seem as if the walls are made of corrugated cardboard, like the flaps on a carton, inside out.

There's a movement in a front-facing window. The gauzy white curtains had stirred—it's the window of Mrs. Kamsky's parlor. I hesitate on the sidewalk, mumbling to myself, and calling myself stupid, when I realize that Mrs. Kamsky is standing by the curtain, watching me. Oh, everything is tidy and attractive. There are flower beds in the usual way, and a shiny green lawn, and high old shade trees, and a good wood fence across the back, with four old willows along it, and their branches are like thin green hair. The two big azaleas at the sides of Mrs. Kamsky's front steps are blooming madly, even though it's barely now spring, one white and one pink, and the trees along the street will soon begin opening flowers: there are dogwoods, horse chestnuts, tulip trees, red-budded maples, and ash. The sky is lower than in town, and much bluer—but we are higher up the valley, nearer to the hills. If twenty elephants, made of pure white meringue, were walking slow-motion in a circle, close to each other, but not touching, then that would be the look of the clouds.

I walk up the short sidewalk to her door. I do not want her thinking of me as a coward.

But I would have appreciated a different house, more in line with my expectations, as vague as they were. More height, I would have wanted: more height, more light, and more air. And there should have been personal touches and a little more flair, instead of grayness, blandness, and sameness, so you'd have some indication right away that the person who lived here was not what you would have expected.

Here is Mrs. Kamsky in the doorway.

"Do come in, although my friend didn't tell me what your name is."

"That's because he didn't ask me."

"Do come in."

"It's Margaret," I tell her. "Margaret Dunlap."

"Are you called something else? Peg, or Peggy? Or Maggie?"

"I'm called Margaret."

I look at her, this first time, not completely, not directly, but in pieces, out the sides of my eyes. In a burst of terrible prescience, as if she lived a secret life as a clairvoyant, Mrs. Kamsky could whirl about and find me out. She could fling back her head and shake her fists in the air, and cry out, "You're an imposter! I see right through you! You are a liar! Get out of my house!"

This does not take place. It's my conscience, rising up to remind me that it is there. It's bristly and prickly, and pushes against the underside of my skin, and the only thing to say to it is, "Go away."

When I enter the quiet house I feel a little less uneasy. I feel lucky to be not very tall. I am five feet three inches, and Mrs. Kamsky is even smaller—she is shorter than me by half a head.

She is round and pudgy—not fat, exactly, but fleshy and oval and dense, along the lines of an owl. I'm glad to see that she is not the sort of person who believes in using hair dye. She's completely gray, and not softly, either. She is gray like a scouring pad; she wears her hair very short, in the style that used to be called a "pixie." My guess is, she cuts it herself (and I'm right).

There's nothing flabby or soft or weak or sickly about her hands, which are long and strong. Her eyes are light blue, and small and sharp and intelligent and shiny. Her complexion is so fair, you could tell that, before she lost her color, her hair had been blond.

Her outfit is appalling. She wears a sweatsuit, of pants and a zippered sweatshirt—not the kind with a hood, but with a natty little collar, like on a golf shirt. She couldn't have done this on purpose, but the color of the suit is exactly the same as the pink azalea on her stoop. Even worse, the suit is velvet, crushed velvet, the last thing in the world that any normal person would want to sweat in. It must have come from a rack, in an expensive department store, that said, "Outfits to Lounge Around Your House In." But it doesn't have, like you see sometimes on these types of clothes, rhinestones or little jewel specks, along the pockets and trim.

She is barefoot. Her feet are dirty and gray, as if she'd been walking in dust, and the dust had caked in deeply.

There does not seem to be anything wrong with Mrs. Kamsky. Oh, she would need to have her meals designed carefully, she would need to be put on a diet, but that seems to be all.

Which hip is the false one, you can't tell. She stands firmly on her own two legs. The pinkish flush in her cheeks isn't makeup. It's normal slightly flushed healthy skin.

I had prepared myself for an invalid, but when my first impressions begin to register with me, I realize that Mrs. Kamsky is probably stronger, and more generally vigorous, than I am. If a stranger passed her front door, glanced inside, and had to choose which one of us was the patient, no one except God would ever have chosen correctly.

"Margaret," I say to myself. "More is going on here than meets the eye."

From the short front hall, I can see into all the rooms: dining room to the right, parlor to the left, bedroom down a second short hall, and kitchen straight ahead. There is very little furniture. No pictures are on the walls, no photographs, no mail, no magazines, no clutter, no anything. These rooms are clean and impersonal, like rooms in a suburban motel.

But something is strange about the kitchen.

It looks smaller than it should; the proportions are wrong. The back wall, which faces the beautiful willows, has no windows. The wall is covered with inexpensive, dark paneling, and the cracks in the paneling, at the end of the counter, are in fact not cracks at all.

In front of my eyes, the cracks take the shape of a door frame. A single straight line—a fissure of light—appears down the length of the wall, as thin as a string. It slowly, steadily widens.

I wouldn't have guessed that the door was there, until it opened. Mrs. Kamsky says, "Oh, for Pete's sake, my pupils," and it seems that she's talking, for some reason, about her eyes.

But coming in the kitchen through that door, ducking low, is a boy, a big, light-haired, fair-skinned boy, about fourteen or fifteen years old. And behind him comes another boy, and another, and then another. How they fit together in that tiny kitchen, with all the stuff they're carrying, backpacks, gym bags, and duffels, I don't know. They are dressed like anyone else their age: baseball caps on backward, T-shirts, loose old drab green Army surplus pants, as baggy on those legs as the pants of clowns. They arrange themselves along the length of the kitchen in a row, shoulder to shoulder. There are gaps in between each boy of just a couple of inches. They are all very fit and very tall; their heads are higher than the tops of the cabinets.

In their presence, Mrs. Kamsky looks as small and round as a dumpling. She says to me, "How much did my friend explain to you?"

"Your friend was in a hurry. But if I had to put a number on it, I'd put a zero."

"That's what I thought. I told them to stay where they were, and leave quietly the back way, but they've never done anything I've told them before, so, why should something be different?" Then she says to the boys, "This is the lady from the health care agency."

They take a long time before replying, as if they're pupils in a sign language class, each one as deaf as a nail: Mrs. Kamsky could have been teaching them to lip-read.

But no, they have all of the usual senses. "You staying?" says a boy. It's the second boy to have appeared, and the youngest. He is lanky and thin like a colt, with a colt's wide eyes, but his ease on his legs and in his body, just like the others, is the same as a grown-up horse's. There is a military bearing about him—about them all, as if their chins are propped up with invisible yardsticks, as if wires or harnesses, not muscles and bones, hold back their shoulders.

They make it look like this is natural. You never notice, in the ordinary world, how normal it is for everyone to walk around slouching, just slouching and slumping around, until you come upon people who don't. It's a startling thing. Your eyes need a moment to adjust. "I only just got here," I say to the second boy.

Another boy says, "Hey, like, good luck."

This is the way they take leave of Mrs. Kamsky: she stands by the front door, and each one, passing her, pauses, and sets down whatever he's carrying, and holds out his hands to her. Mrs. Kamsky inclines her face upward and is kissed on each cheek, in such an easy, natural gesture, I have to say to myself, "They look it, and they sound it, but I cannot believe that these boys are Americans."

They don't quite bow to Mrs. Kamsky, but they give the impression that they are bowing to her. They pick up their bags and go out the front door and I start to miss them as soon as the door closes behind them.

If I never saw the moon before, not even in pictures, and no one had told me that it existed, and then suddenly one

night I came upon it—I looked up and started staring at it
—would I know what it was? Would some instinct kick in
to let me know? If I looked for the first time ever at a half
or a quarter of it, would I know that the rest was hidden?

I think I would, just like anyone else. You wouldn't need
to stop and think about it. You wouldn't have to know ahead
of time what the word for it was: you would see it, and you
would know it as the moon, without the word.

And you would know the same way that those four boys
were dancers. You would know what they did with Mrs.
Kamsky in that room behind the kitchen before anyone mentioned, "ballet."

I say to myself, "I think this is something I could put
up with." I do not consider that what I had done was fraudu-
lent. Did I ask for this? Did I submit, or even create, a false
resume? I'd done nothing of the kind, and no one had asked
me for one. I think of myself as honest and fair. I think of
my heart, like anyone else's, as a container of two different
forces, one hard and one soft, like layers of water and wood,
which are sometimes unequal in strength, and are sometimes, somehow, in the right conditions, aligned with each
other in balance. Or as Mrs. Kamsky would put it, as she
puts it so often, in her usual thoughtful, tactful way, "Margaret was like a mule all her life, she was absolutely a mule,
until she turned up one day on my doorstep and saw my
boys."

AS FOR MY Greek neighbor, she recovered from her illness
and went back to work.

I saw her from time to time in our hallway, and she'd look
at me fondly and say, no matter what season we were in, "It's
good that winter is over," and then she'd say, "Next week
when I pay the gas bill, I will pay you twenty dollars."

"No," I'd answer. "I won't take it, I have a new job," and she would touch my arm and say, in the same tone of voice, like an echo of herself, "Next week when I pay the gas bill, I will pay you twenty dollars."

Then one day my neighbor was gone. I did not inquire about her. It could have happened that she went to live in a Greek-speaking nursing home in another town; or she'd gone back to where she'd come from, to Athens, I imagined. Some relative of hers could have loaned her the money for an airplane ticket and there she must have been, in a quiet Greek room with big, clean windows, on a high white classical hill, looking out on an ocean where gods used to live, where foam along the waves, I imagine, is like whiskers of old, dead gods.

ACTUALLY, in my first few weeks, I was tempted many times to tell Mrs. Kamsky about Mrs. Panadopolous.

I would have enjoyed describing what the sunlight was like on the wrecks of the fleet in the old bus graveyard, just a couple of hours before I first met her, as if that was why I noticed the light, and then suddenly, there were bits of white light everywhere, like white sparks, and even the rust on those buses, to my eyes, although I didn't know why at the time, was lovely and coppery and glowing, like illuminated honey and mustard. I also would have told her about the feet of my neighbor and how she could not wear laces in her shoes.

The furthest I ever got in any sort of confession was just after a packing routine one morning—the second one of the day, it had been, not counting her ice-down, which always took place after breakfast.

The packs lay in secret at the center of her life. I was moved to speak honestly because finally, I was beginning to get the hang of working them. I was able to tell in the course of the day, just by looking, when it was time to use ice, whether soft-frozen gel packs, or faster-working ice cubes, or it was time to use heat, either gels, electric pads, or old-fashioned hot-water bottles, which could also serve as cushions for elevation, and were good for the knees.

Refinements in my methods, such as knowing when to bully her, and when to back off, would come to me later. I learned very quickly when to wrap the packs tightly, and when not to.

Ice-downs were for the swellings that occurred in the night, every night, while she slept. They took place in her bathtub and involved one hundred forty-four ice cubes, from the dozen trays that were always kept filled in her kitchen freezer. She asked me once to never look at the expression on her face when I helped her lower herself into a tub of ice cubes, and I never did. The only thing about the ice-downs that was tolerable was that, when they were over, we would both have the knowledge that, no matter what else happened, the day ahead of us could only get better.

Anyway, her packing system was so intricate, even a health care aide with many years of experience would have a hard time in learning to help her, without acting as if, at the ends of your arms, there were paws instead of hands, or thumbs instead of fingers, and you were causing more damage than what was there, which in spite of Mrs. Kamsky's illusions, was a lot. So I said to her one day, in a burst of self-confidence, "I'm finally getting the hang of all this, but I think I'd better tell you that I haven't been working as a health care aide for very long," and she answered, "Oh, I would never be able to guess, but let me tell you something that will make you feel better," and my moment of truth passed us by. Afterward it would always feel too late, the way you don't need to be talking about the trouble you took before to make a nice evening meal, while now, you're sitting there eating the meal.

She said, "What do you call the dummies set up on the field, when boys practice football? The boys rush at the big blocks of dummies and ram into them and try to tackle them?"

I didn't know. I said, "Practice tackler dummies."

"There is someone, a ballerina, not here now, but from before. After a surgery she was given an aide who lasted with her not even five minutes," said Mrs. Kamsky.

Something was in her voice that I hadn't heard there before. I pricked up my ears to it, the way you'd notice it if someone who never sang to you before, suddenly began singing. A ballerina. From before. "Not here."

There had never been a "before" with Mrs. Kamsky. I had figured it out already that in the world, there are people who are people in the world, and then there are people in dancing.

There is only one way for people in dancing to know about time, which is, it is now.

There is now, now, and more now. There is now, this minute, right now. There is now, now, now, now, today, this hour, this instant, this heartbeat, this pulse beat, all now, because everything that matters is here and now: there isn't anything else, just now. You should always think twice about it when dancers talk about "before." They are always only speaking of now, and this isn't just true of Mrs. Kamsky, although Mrs. Kamsky seems to take it to extremes.

"This aide," she was saying, "had a previous job as a practice tackler, but she couldn't be called a dummy, as she could speak. She was also a woman gorilla, and she was also a former Marine, all in one. It was very upsetting and the ballerina would never allow herself to try again with a different aide."

I said, "What did she do?"

"I imagine she went back to the Marines," said Mrs. Kamsky.

"No, I mean the other one."

"The ballerina? Ah, the ballerina became married to her surgeon."

The *ballerina*. She said "ballerina" as though she wasn't speaking English to me, bal air een ah, with an accent going deeply on the *een,* and with her voice holding onto it and drawing it out. I thought of the way Italians, real Italians, not Americans, put perfect small pauses, like the pause between beats of a pulse, between the "spa" and the "get," and the "get" and the "tee," when saying "spaghetti," and you know that everything they want to say about their feelings, past and present, comes across in the pauses, somehow, loud and clear. I heard the very smallest of pauses between the last two syllables of Mrs. Kamsky's "ballerina." In the pause, was a world.

Now there are words that stay above our heads in the air, like actual things, not moving, not floating, just there. They are as real as though, if you looked at the wall behind them, you'd be surprised to see them casting no shadows: bal air een ah, and then, "not here now."

lisette

MY IMP WAS HERE last night and I thought it might have left me for good. It's been a long time since I saw it.

"So dance for me. So show me what you think you can do."

It sat on the windowsill with its usual flickering. There was the usual smug demeanor, as one would expect. There was the usual, blue-jay-like tipping of its head. In size, it's as small as a cricket.

"Hi, there, Lisette, I'm your imp, Hi, there, Lisette, I'm your imp," said over and over, is the only attempt at speech it ever made that I could recognize.

It's jumpy although it never once moves. It's as bright as a flame. It sits there as though its body is made of a candlestick, and in its tiny bright eyes there are wicks that somehow were lit, and they are steadily burning, against all the rules of nature.

My imp. It keeps me awake until three, until four, until five, until the gray light of morning comes in. It neatly crosses its knees, and looks dapper and cocky and spry, like a three-inch Fred Astaire, or like the cricket in a Disney cartoon. There are many different aspects of it that I am fond of.

"So don't just sit there. Come a little closer."

I know what will happen if I try to touch it. It will be gone as if nothing was there.

One day my second daughter ran outdoors with the camera because a chipmunk was sitting on our woodpile. It was eating a bulb that it had just dug up from the garden. She had wanted a photo of a chipmunk. It was sitting there perfectly calmly as she aimed the camera and clicked, and it had seemed to her that it was still right there when she went back in the house, but when the film was developed, what came out was a photo of our pile of wood. She kept looking and looking at it for the chipmunk. She thought there was something wrong with her eyes.

I PROMISED my husband and older daughter (the younger one being too young) that I will never leave the house at night when they are sleeping and go out and drive around, which they never would have discovered if, one time, I had not parked the car again, what, six inches from where my child, who has a gift of geometry, remembered her father having left it.

Really, I don't go anywhere far, and it's perfectly safe. I just go out and drive around through the streets, mostly in summer. Sometimes I look at a river, which passes by the edge of this town.

MARGARET HAD CALLED me on the phone last week to say, "Good luck, Lisette," and I told her, "I'm not Lisette anymore. Please remember this. I'm Lisa now."

NOW I'VE RECEIVED from Margaret an eight-page letter, an encouraging, helpful letter, in warm tones, agreeing that, in starting out as I am, in a life of my own, taking pupils of my own, as far away from Mrs. Kamsky as I could get, while continuing to remain in America, well, everything I'd said to Margaret was right: everything Mrs. Kamsky ever taught me had been designed by Mrs. Kamsky, under cover of affection and concern, to destroy me.

Margaret advises me to remember most of all what it was like for me to ever have tried to please Mrs. Kamsky—did I recall what it was like, having done things to disappoint her? How her shoulders turned inward, how her eyes filled with blankness, like the eyes of a victim of shock? Her unhappiness took her over like a miserable, perhaps permanent change in the weather.

She never raised her voice in those moods: why should Mrs. Kamsky need a voice? A cloud of gloom would come round her, shutting me out. She had hoped so much to discover in me a person descended from angels, not apes.

Margaret urges me on. "Do everything different! Whatever you learned from Irene, ball it up and throw it into a pit!" She urges me to try starting freshly, with my own ways of doing things, with a fresh, clean slate. "My dear Margaret," I wrote back, "I'm doing great."

I SAID TO HER one day, "I'm not learning more Russians from you," and she looked at me as if I had struck her with the back of my hand. "But I thought you liked them."

"I liked them very much until you started to make me dance them. You didn't have to tell me that all Russian music is for dancing at the edge of a pit, and inside the pit is black despair, that's what you said, if it's Russian, then somewhere nearby, there's a pit of despair."

"You want shallow? You want pretty little Italians? You want to look as if you came off of a cake? You want to dance like a pretty decoration on a cake? You want French? You want Giselle? You know what is wrong with Giselle? Giselle has no spine. Giselle has no forgive me for being vulgar, balls. You want no balls?"

"But I'm a girl," I said.

"Metaphorical balls is what I meant. You don't want them? Then stay away from the Russians, I agree with you."

"But I liked it when the best thing to hear in the music was the horses in the snow, with sleigh bells on, and you took that away from me. You ruined that pleasure for me completely."

"Oh, if all you want is horses and bells, and a sleigh ride and a nice fur muff, I'll play louder when the horses go by, and you can have a nice moment of comfort. You can say to yourself, 'I'm so glad because, Doctor Boris Zhivago is the man I am falling in love with, he's handsome, oh I dream of him all day long.'"

"His name isn't Boris," I said.

MY OLDER DAUGHTER came up with a plan to get more pupils: she thinks I should advertise my classes in the newspaper here, a thing I'd never do. And she thinks the ad should mention the fact that I'm married to an orthopedic surgeon.

"Orthopedic surgeon on the premises," she thinks it should say. This afternoon before my children came home from school I lay down on the couch and cried for half an hour. Maybe it was longer.

I SAID TO HER one day, because I was frightened of many things, and of one thing especially, "A girl in my apartment building went crazy last Friday and her family came and took her away. She was fine and then all of a sudden she was screaming and seeing things on the walls that weren't there. She'd been going to some kind of art school. She had the room under mine. I didn't see anything happen. But I heard about it. I was halfway ready to pack up and move out, just hearing about it, and she's not even one of my friends."

"It's not contagious," my teacher answered. "It's not going to seep up through your floor, you know, like a gas leak."

"How did you know that's what I thought?"

"Because to dance can make you walk on the edge of being crazy, every minute, all the time, and also, when I was your age," she said, "I had a room just like it, so I was there."

ONE HAS ONE'S PUPILS, which, on its own, as I'm beginning to see, is quite enough. One can stop dancing when it is time, and have a full, rich life, and be a part of the world. As for the dancing, I have always been able to look at myself very frankly. But I wish I could have had it a little longer.

In the old days, before my life was divided in two separate parts, before and after dancing, I'd lie down at night and go happily to that place between awake and asleep, as if it were an actual place you can go to.

In the moments before sleeping takes over, where shapes move and glisten with life of their own, there'd be things that would zip to the surface and display themselves, from the hodge-podge of every known thing.

I saw marvelous pictures. A shiny red bicycle would be parked plain as day on a beach, in foamy, breaking waves, but it would never fall over. A yapping white dog would run by, but its head would be the head of a cabbage.

In the lake of dreams, carpets in my hall were really swimming pools; clowns from a circus drove fire engines; an orchestra put their instruments down and played a game of Monopoly, then said, "We're tired of this, let's make love," and threw off their clothes and started kissing each other, and I was there, too.

In the dance "Petrouchka," which I could see as if it were playing behind my eyes, the puppet looked like a girl, and climbed into a spacecraft, like an astronaut, dripping wet, as naked as a girl stepping out from a shower, and the girl is me, and around my shoulders, just like a picture in a book, were the rings of the planet Saturn.

A splinter of wood, tilting this way and that in a bowl of gray water, would change to a seahorse as small as a thumb, with a real horse's head, which would leap in the air and turn into a candle; but the wax of the candle was really the stuff from a breast, when there isn't quite milk, when the baby is one hour old.

On and on it used to go, like dances: colors bright as neon, nightly parades, everything shifting and changing, then put back together, somehow, as something else.

But now, wherever I look, there's a hole.

Or the imp turns up with its flickering. The imp. Its heart is made of fire. "I'm your imp, I'm your imp."

THE STREETLIGHT by the front of our house is shining like it always does through my yellow and white striped curtains. Wind chimes, like thin aluminum pistons, hang from a hook on the porch. I try to catch sound of them, but there isn't any wind.

MY HUSBAND does not worry that perhaps I might miss my old life. Does the puppet who broke away from its strings miss its strings?

His body beside me is something I take for granted. He knows nothing about the imp. I don't want to feel far away from him, so I roll to my side and touch his arm near his elbow; my fingers there are like half of a bracelet. Holding his arm is like holding a railing, while walking down rickety stairs. I know that at the bottom of the staircase is sleep, but it takes a long time to get down there.

Our daughters are too big to be in bed with us but I picture them here anyway, settling down quickly, in a way they would never have done in real life. In real life, they would have begged for glasses of water, demanded to have their backs rubbed, fought with each other; they would have wakened their father by jumping on him and pinching his nose. Even in the dark, I would have noticed their dandruff and ear wax, their furtive, guilty expressions, the scabs they never stopped picking, a neck that hadn't been washed, a tooth that was growing in crooked, their fingernail dirt and faint smells of pee. I would have seen all those things a mother sees every day, and tries to never make a big deal of. I'd say to myself, "Now I am a mother."

I imagine my children as meek as puppets. The back of the head of the older one is between my breasts; the younger one, straddling my hip, squirms for a moment, then falls asleep like a baby in a saddle.

Everyone on earth is sleeping but me.

I TRY TO SEE things again, in that light behind my eyes—imagined, I know, but very real, like anything that thrives in different light, like mushrooms shut away in a cellar, or like a letter you write that's never slid into an envelope, that no one will ever read.

Aren't there houses that people build carefully, of loving detail, of wood that never came from a tree, on land that never existed? I think about this.

Aren't there songs people sing, that no ear ever heard, and long conversations of one voice only, and paintings that were never put onto a canvas?

Aren't there lovers who will never see each other again, long-distance swimmers who never go into the water, bowls by potters who never sat down at a wheel, meals by chefs who never cooked, and conductors of trains that never moved on actual steel?

I think that these things must be everywhere. There must be millions of pictures, moving and standing still, like dances, now and tomorrow and always, unseen, but completely natural and normal.

Yes, these things must be everywhere, like bits of invisible light, like air, like fire you can feel but not see, like quiet,

37

watchful cats in the moonlight by a window, looking out at the night with the hearts of lynxes and tigers, dreaming of brave, strong things.

THE DANCES I IMAGINED when I was young were full of trees. The backdrop was always trees. I had loved writing stage notes. I had wanted other people to see what I saw.

What other people? There were no other people.

"Buds as white as snow are on the apple trees. This is the day when buds are poking up on old stems in an apple orchard, and a lonesome ballerina named Lisette comes out by herself to see them."

"The color of the light when we first see the ballerina is very white, and in it, that is, under it, there is an underlining of the palest shade of green that you can have, like moonlight on trees, when spring is just starting, but the branches are covered with snow (and apple blossoms too)."

A NEW PUPIL, a girl of eleven, clever and daring and coarse and a prankster (but not a good dancer), wrote me a love note. It conveniently happened to fall from the pocket of her coat onto the doorstep.

"My dancing teacher is so arrogunt. The first thing she teaches you is that, everything you do, is like mannore. But you shouldn't take it the wrong way. The next thing you get to learn is, how not to make it stink."

I SAY TO MY PUPILS, "This is what we do. We want our souls to show themselves through some things that a body can do, which is a little like saying that, through a hole in a window shade about the size of a pinpoint, when the shade's pulled all the way down, you can make out a pinpoint of sunlight."

I never look directly in anyone's face when I talk like this.

WHEN THE STAR of my fortunes had fallen—and I had seen this plainly, unsentimentally, as it was happening—the worst of it was, I saw that there was never a star at all, just a meteorite. This is a nicer way of saying "a rock," as in, "I had started out so hopefully, but my chances in life, it turned out, were like the chances of an old gray dead rock."

"I WOULD LIKE to make you a small suggestion. I wonder what would come of it, if, perhaps this one time, as a small variation, you thought of something to do a little differently."

"What do you want me to do?"

"I believe it would be good for us all if you gave us some help in fighting the desire to fall fast asleep, when we come here to watch you. You could hurry to us and pinch us, you know, when we start nodding off, or you could say that there are bells around your neck. If there are bells around your neck, my dear, a very good time to be shaking them would be now."

"Bells like sleigh bells?"

"Jingle jingle jingle! It's very cold. If we fall asleep sitting in one place like this, we will soon be frozen like lamb chops."

DO I REMEMBER what it was like to try to please her? I do. The effort to please Mrs. Kamsky was like walking in mud.

EVERY DANCE I imagine lately has a giant man with an ax. It's a sort of roadblock. I am trying to get past this image. All that happens with the giant and his ax is that he strides around in a forest and now and then chops down a tree. This is not a good idea for a dance.

THE HUMAN FOOT has many small bones. There are dancers who never break any of them. There are dancers who break a few. There are dancers who break them all. I met my husband in a clinic. He held my feet in his hands.

I sat on a table in an exam room. He was in front of me, sitting on a silver stool: a white-coated big black-haired man from Colorado, a man who loves to ski, a man who takes up a lot of space and fills it with his own husky health and well-being, a man who goes striding into the world every day in a big wool jacket like a picture of the famous lumberjack giant Paul Bunyan, come to life from out of a storybook.

He had a stethoscope—not Paul Bunyan's big ax. He smelled like outside, even in the air of the clinic. He took hold of my feet and held them in the palms of his hands. His fingers curved up around my heels like the backs of shoes. Then he touched my toes with the tips of his fingers, lightly, lightly.

I wasn't asking myself if he were someone I thought I might "love." I was asking myself if he were someone who could try to fix my feet.

I was his first ballerina. He must have seen pictures of what feet of a dancer are like, in textbooks, in pathology classes.

He shouldn't have had the shock that he had when he looked at my feet. I felt sorry for him. Tears filled his eyes the way eyes go suddenly teary when you go outside into sub-zero cold. He had thought for a moment that I had suffered from frostbite.

I didn't marry him because he's a physician, or because I felt sorry for him, or because his specialty is orthopedics. I married him because he asked me to, and he smelled like outdoors.

SOMETIMES IT SEEMS I'm just about ready to reach into the bag in my mind that holds everything I ever knew about dancing. Reaching into it would mean that the giant and his ax were out of the way and I was making up a new dance.

It might mean that this is something after all I really would do. I could feel it sometimes—the urge of it—like a word on the tip of your tongue that you can't seem to get. It's like the feeling you're about to sneeze and then you don't.

Sometimes it's really that simple. But then I can't quite reach the bag, or I can't quite get it to open. Or something will flicker in a corner of the room. When I turn to see what it is, nothing's there. "Nothing's there," I say to myself. "Don't be always looking for what you know is not there."

MY IMP. "Dance for me. Show me something new. Show me something I want to look at. Show me something to make my heart jump."

It sits there. "Hi, there, Lisette, I'm your imp." A flame. A fiery bit of sharpness and brightness in the shadows.

THERE'S BEEN ANOTHER letter from Margaret to say that she wouldn't blame me if it never once occurs to me to wonder what Mrs. Kamsky, lately, might be up to. I should take it for granted that she would have no more tricks up her sleeves. "Margaret," I wrote back, "I never think about her at all."

THE SUBURB where she finally settled is an awful little place of houses that all look the same, like on a TV show. She liked the camouflage it gave her. She thinks that everything there is to know about me, she knows it, but she is wrong.

THE HOUSE my husband and I settled on is what is known here as a split-level ranch. We chose it for its big backyard, which made it easier for me to have an addition put on, which is now my studio.

Before we bought it, my husband and I and our daughters had looked at a Victorian, which stuck out dramatically in these miles and miles of buildings lying low to the ground.

We seemed destined to buy it at once. We walked through the rooms in a state of marvel; my husband and I, whispering secretly to each other, imagining that the house in its earlier life had been a brothel; we imagined that the walls were coated with opium smoke. Then the real estate agent who was showing us the house stuck a pin in our fantasies. "Doesn't it look authentic, for something that's only been standing here a few months?"

ON A TABLE, there's a bowl of salad. I pick out some lettuce, and I put the lettuce on a plate. I cut up the lettuce with a knife and fork as one would cut food for a child, except, I'm the child. Someone—I don't know who—says, "Why did you cut up your lettuce in tiny pieces?" I answer, "My teacher told me to." But nothing like this had ever taken place in real life.

I NEVER SAY to my pupils, "My feet broke, so I have to be careful, and that is why I sit on a stool when I am teaching you."

I say, "I sit while I am teaching you because I can see you better this way."

I say, "All the best dancing teachers always sit."

IT WASN'T AS IF all the bones broke at once. Some of them were broken while others were on the mend. Some took a longer time to break at all. My husband was never taken to a ballet when he was young and he has still never been to one, and when movies like *Oklahoma!* and *West Side Story* are playing on our video machine, he gets up and leaves the room every time the dancing lasts longer than a minute, or he picks up a pillow and puts it over his eyes.

Our daughters play T-ball and soccer. They turn up the radio and pretend to play guitars in a band. They want to grow up to be surgeons.

I'M AN ASTRONAUT. A launch is about to take place. I'm suited up; I go into the hatch. I take my seat in the capsule. The countdown starts. Suddenly, I remember something. It's not a specific thing. "I'm sorry, but, I can't go for this ride," I tell everyone. I take off my helmet. I leave that capsule and go back into the arms of real gravity.

IN ANOTHER DREAM, I'm teaching a class, the class is going along. There's a girl in here, about twenty. I never saw her before. She looks like she never washes her hair, and she slouches down low in her backbone, in that way they have sometimes, as if, if you try to teach them anything they have to fight for, they will only fight you, instead, and will hate you. When I say something the girl doesn't like, she gives me the finger, straight up. The other pupils feel anxious and worried about this. Then it's the end of the year: I've finished with most of them, except the ones I will retain for private classes, which I've decided to be picky about. It's a very dramatic moment: I'm going around to each pupil, whispering into their ear if they've been chosen. It's the turn of the girl I don't like, who expects to find her name at the top of my list.

I whisper, "You're busted, scumbag." The tone of my voice, and my expression in general, are exactly like those of the police on *Hill Street Blues,* a television show that is now off the air. But it's my husband's favorite show, for some reason, and he's got all the episodes on tape, and watches them over and over, to relax to.

MY HUSBAND and I went out to see a movie at the multiplex in our nearby shopping mall. The ushers, boys as well as girls, as a one-time promotional gimmick for a film that was opening, were dressed in tuxedos. "Oh, what a good idea, you should do this all the time," I said to the boy who tore our tickets.

He said, "They made us pay the rentals ourselves, and if we sweat too much, we have to buy them."

SAY THAT THERE IS a builder of chairs who goes into a workshop every day and makes chairs. He was supposed to make chairs that are sittable-on, and will match in a set, but he keeps on making chairs that have three legs instead of four, or chairs that don't feel comfortable.

He never quite made them to match. Each chair was as unique as a snowflake. He used unpopular types of wood and painted them in colors you would not expect to find in a chair. Naturally, no one wanted to buy them except a few people close to the chair-builder (he has a few well-off neighbors).

Sometimes the builder rents a booth at a crafts fair, displays a few chairs, and feels good for a couple of days afterward. This goes on and on. Finally one day the builder realizes how tired he is, and how his heating bills are getting higher, and how expensive it is to buy the types of materials he favors, and so he has to make a decision. He's getting old. His hands shake. Should he try to forget what he used to be able to do? Can the lines between his hands and his soul be disconnected? Should he set his workshop on fire? Should he buy a TV and a comfortable armchair? Should he sleep all day long? What will become of his hands? Should they be chopped off his arms with an ax?

I THOUGHT OF the ushers in tuxedos for days and days afterward. Now and then a glimmer would move in a corner, or I would suddenly catch my breath, my heart would pound strangely, as if I'd been running, although I'd been standing perfectly still. It would seem to me that I had seen the ushers in a dream. They were local high school boys with part-time jobs as ushers. Not dancers. In the lobby of the movie theater in real life, they had not been taking tickets in fifth

position, they had not been striking poses, they had not
squared their shoulders, they had not picked a foot off the
floor. But that was what I remembered them doing.

THERE WAS A CARNIVAL in a nearby town. I went with my
husband and both of our daughters. It was a splendid spring
afternoon, a Sunday. But the carnival was a cheap affair and
had no spirit, without anyone doing anything except going
through the motions and just getting another day over with.
All the workers looked sad and exhausted and had unhealthy
skin and hollow expressions and empty eyes. There were
three or four elephants. A petting zoo, in a small fenced area,
contained goats. There were also several monkeys, and some
ponies. I looked at these animals and I felt I was reading their
thoughts, and I said to myself, "They wish they could all just
be shot." Then I looked around at the other customers of this
carnival, most of whom, like my husband and me, had come
here to do something as a family, and I thought the same
thing, and felt afraid. Our younger daughter said to us, "I
changed my mind about a pony ride." When we started to
walk back to our car, she said to her sister, "What's the matter with Mommy?" And I heard her sister say, "She misses her
old friends."

"But I thought she didn't like them anymore," said the
younger one. "You don't have to like your friends," said her
sister. "You just have to have some."

My husband gave me a look. I whispered to him, "They
get these ideas from watching television, not from me."

IT DOES ME NO GOOD to keep counting my losses. Like Lot's
wife, I'll change into a pillar if I think about things that had
not gone the way they were supposed to. My mouth will fill
with salt, my hair will be stone, my throat will close up, and

I'll dangle in spirit outside of myself, flattened and trapped, like a shadow thrown out from a statue. As my husband says, if fate deals you lemons, then get ice cubes, sugar, water, and a pitcher, and enjoy your lemonade, or else break a few open and suck them, and sit around all day and make faces and say, "Everything in life is so sour."

SHE LOVED stories of the Trojan War. It was one of those things about her that I was allowed to know. She told me once that she was afraid she would die before she understood a way to show, with her body, what it was like in the days after Troy had been destroyed.

She had wanted me to read books, to find out about Troy. "Please go and find out for yourself what I'm talking about when I talk to you about Troy," she would say, and I'd answer, "Don't be giving me homework."

To put up resistance to her was to say, "Mrs. Kamsky, I'm Lisette. Mrs. Kamsky, I'm Lisette."

I HAD A DREAM that took place in the future. In it, this is what I do for a living: I go around to people's houses as a tutor and teach their small children what the parts of their bodies are. That's what I do. I walk around someone's living room with a boy about sixteen months old. I touch the tip of his nose. "Nose," I say. "A nose is part of your face." "Face," I say. "A face is a part of your head." I seem to be successful at this work. I'm in demand, I'm listed in the phone book. When I leave this house, the child will have been properly taught; then I'll go to another house and do the same. "Elbow," I say. "Your elbow is part of your arm."

THERE WAS ONLY one other time that my husband looked at feet that made him cry.

They were the feet of an elderly Chinese woman. She was eighty or ninety, a small, small woman. She was the grandmother of someone my husband had known in medical school. The grandson had brought her to America. He brought her himself into my husband's clinic. He had tried to get the grandson to tell him the Mandarin word for "mutilated," so he could say it to the woman, but the grandson said, "there is no such translation for that if you are wishing to speak of feet." She walked in tiny, short steps, as if her ankles were handcuffed together. When it was time for her to get up on the exam table, the grandson lifted her and placed her on it as gently as if she were glass. The grandson spoke to her, then translated what he'd said. "I told her that the doctor is standing here crying because he's happy to meet the grandmother of his friend."

The old woman wore thongs (although it was winter) and big white puffy socks. My husband started to cry before the socks were off. When the socks came off, he looked away. "Bound feet" and "ballerina" in my husband's mind are the exact same thing, in two different languages, in two different alphabets.

IN OUR BACKYARD GARDEN which is tended by my husband and our younger daughter (the older one had dug the rows and laid out the design) there've been strawberries and rhubarb; the flowers are healthy; there are squashes on complicated, woody vines.

Each evening when the garden's in season, my husband goes out of the house with our younger daughter, and the two of them pour Black Label beer into plastic containers for the slugs, who drown in great numbers.

I've thought of a method myself, and urge them to try it but they never do: when you find a slug, pick it up with a stick, lay it on a large, flat rock, place a second large rock on top of it, and stand on the second rock.

ONE DAY she said to me, "Go into the kitchen and see if you can
find the big sponge in the cabinet under the sink, the sponge
for washing the car." I went into the kitchen. I found the
sponge. She called out from the studio, "Do you also see the
basin? Fill the basin halfway with water, put the sponge in, and
bring it in here." I did so. "Are we going to wash your car?" "If
we were going to wash my car, we'd be going outdoors." She
kept a car because she liked to have something that was real
and simple, to love and admire. Even when she was living in
the city, even when the time had come for her (physically) to
never drive a car again, she had, she has, an expensive sportscar—it always has to be an antique, and foreign, and red. Usu-
ally it's a handsome little MG. The models changed from time
to time as she was always looking for variations and good
trades, but she always had one, and if you ever read a Nancy
Drew book, you would call it, as I did, her little roadster.

I brought her the basin of the water and the sponge. I set it
on the floor. The sponge absorbed the water and we watched
it swell up, and rise up above the basin like bread dough. She
said, "What would it feel like to you if this is what the ground
of all the earth was really made of?"

"But it's not. It's rocks and ice and hard stuff."

"Imagine."

"It would feel really good."

Then she told me to take my shoes off and stand on the
sponge in the basin, and I did. She said, "Starting this moment,
for people like you, this is what the ground of all the earth is
really made of," and I had believed her.

Unlike most teachers, she never used accompanists; she
played her own piano. I think it's because she didn't want
anyone there except *dancers*. I think I know why.

Sometimes when I was dancing in a room where she was, I
mean specifically when she was at the piano, I had the feeling

that there was, in the room with us, other presences. Sometimes at the barre I would catch odd glimpses of shapes and shadows and I would not understand what they were.

Sometimes when I was dancing alone for Mrs. Kamsky, and sometimes when she was with me out on the floor, showing me something, we weren't alone, and I could not make her see how it felt to me to be able to feel this. When shapes in a room are on a wall, they are ordinary things we call shadows, but what can you call it when shapes flung up on the walls—and shapes moving this way and that across the floor—aren't dark enough to be shadows, or bright enough to be light?

I would ask her this. I'd try to explain to her what I meant. She would look at me. She would shake her head sadly and wonder why I thought I should try to use words.

Shapes all over the walls? Light, shadows, this way and that across a floor, what's the matter with you? Do you think that these are things to say in words?

AND NOW another letter. "You must kiss your babies and Dr. Zhivago good-bye for a while, and get onto an airplane and come," writes Margaret. "Not that you could possibly be interested in anything going on around here, especially something new."

There's a feeling in my stomach that you get when an elevator begins descending down the hole in the center of a building a little faster than you think it ought to be going. I remember what it was like to feel this way all the time. I used to have a name for it. I used to call it "the urge to be dancing."

"If you want a small piece of advice," writes Margaret, "she said to tell you, a very good time for you to be coming, would be now."

class

HERE IS HOW IT IS with you. You come to me so I can show
you something, and I show you, and you say, no, that's not
what we want you to show us, show us something else, and
I tell you, come back tomorrow. When you do, I show you
the same thing, and you say, no, that isn't what we wanted,
and I say, come back tomorrow again, and when you do, I
show you the same thing, the same thing happens all over.
Then I say the next day, okay, I will show you something different now, and so I have your attention, and I show you the
same thing I showed you yesterday and the day before, and
the day before that, and you say, oh, look at this, this is what
we needed you to teach us all along, why did you have to take
four days? The answer to your question is, you never had
training when you were younger, before you came to me,
and so naturally, you act like you are squid, without a backbone.

We say to her, will you show us your body with your
clothes off, so we can see what we're probably in for? We say,
it wouldn't have to be completely naked. We would show you
no disrespect. We really want to look at your joints.

She says, it's a reasonable thing to ask me for, but if I
showed you my body with my clothes off, you would run away
screaming.

We say, if we ran away anywhere, we would run to a circus. There are first-rate circuses all over the world that would
want us, and she says, life itself is a circus although you're still
too young to understand this. She says, what would you do in
a circus?

51

Be acrobats.

She says, come back tomorrow. When we do, she shows us something new, and we say, that's not what we want you to show us, Mrs. Kamsky, there's no jumping in what you show us, we want to jump.

Come back tomorrow, she says, and we do, and as soon as we see what she shows us, we tell her, this is the same thing we saw already, and we never said to you, a bunch of clowns. We said, acrobats.

She says, first we must know what it means to stand still. Anything with two legs can learn to jump. I am trying to explain this to you. I get nowhere. Come back tomorrow.

And we do, and she shows us the very same thing, and we say, acrobats! Acrobats! Acrobats!

She says, come back tomorrow. When we do, we say to her, are you going to show us the same thing? She says, no, it's different now. Then she doesn't show us anything at all.

She sits on the piano bench with her back to the keys, shutting herself away from us. Please turn around and play us something on the piano, because you're making us afraid, we tell her. She won't budge, she won't look at the keys or turn around, but she knows we're serious, so she reaches her arm backward and plays a few notes, and we say, please don't stop playing, please let us hear a little more, and she plays a few more notes but her heart's not in it.

You're speaking to us in an unusual way, we say to her. We want to know the reason why. We want to know what it is that is obscuring your clarity with us. We want to know what you're doing with us. Why can't you just tell us, do this, or do that? Just tell us what to do and we will do it. Why should anything be different?

She says that she is having some trouble with her hip, not the artificial one, the other one.

At this moment right now, are you in pain?

She says, you must know me well enough by now to know that, if I'd got to the point where I was willing to answer yes to your question, I wouldn't be conscious long enough to answer yes.

We ask her if she is going to die, and she says, not in the next five minutes. We say, do you take morphine?

No, and if I did, she says, I wouldn't need to be here with you trying to teach you something. I would spare myself the trouble. I would be lying in my bed with a very happy smile on my face, watching everything I've ever thought of, every step, danced by angels.

Does it mean you've cheered up, by saying angels would be dancing your steps, instead of devils, and maybe you'll get something done with us today?

I say angels because it's daylight. It's the middle of the afternoon, she says.

We tell her, you're not supposed to be talking to us like this. You're supposed to be making it attractive to us to grow up and want to do this. Then we want to talk about Lisette. Does Lisette take morphine?

That wouldn't be Lisette's style, she says. She is much too fond of vodka.

We would like to see tapes of Lisette dancing. We would like to know if the things you always said about Lisette are true. There must be tapes somewhere and we would very much like to see them.

She says, tell me who, in your opinion, is the one greatest painter who ever lived.

We don't know that much about the subject of painting, and she says, you've been taken to museums and you have eyes, and we say, oh, then for us, there is mainly the great Caravaggio.

A tape of a dance is like Caravaggio on a postcard, she says. A tape of a dance compared to dancing is like a big purple grape compared to a raisin.

We like raisins, we say.

There's no tapes of Lisette, she says.

Are there tapes of you?

There are no tapes of me. There is nothing of me that I can show you except what you see right in front of your eyes every day that you come here.

We say, there must be pictures of when you danced. Cameras were invented already when you danced.

There are no pictures.

Then she tells us that now we would have to go home. She says, go home. I have nothing to teach you today, and stay away because, I will have nothing for you tomorrow.

What about the day after that?

She says, the day after that will be the same.

We say, we are running out of patience here. You promised us that you would make us into dancers. This is what you're here to do. You said we would not grow up to be ordinary people. You chose us to be your pupils. If you're planning to break your promise with us, now would be a pretty good time to let us know.

Now I'm planning on breaking my promise to you, she says.

And we say, well, we never should have got our hopes up with you, seeing what you've done to our hopes.

Hope, she says. Hope is like a bubble on the suds of detergent in my sink.

She says that there are many other teachers for us to go to right here in the valley. We have made it this far. There is no going back to being ordinary. She would make a few phone calls on our behalf to some teachers she knows, so we ask her what to do with everything she had taught us so far.

We ask her, what about the steps you taught us already?

They are yours and you can do what you like with them. Throw them into a hole, she says.

What about the way she taught us to stand, the way she taught us to lift, the way she taught us to talk?

They are all for throwing into a hole.

All right then, we'll be going now, we say.

We have to walk past her to go down to the end of the studio to pick our things up, so we ask her if she thinks she would be able to not look at us when we walk by her.

Maybe, we tell her, you should have put some windows in here. Looking out of windows would help you not look at us.

You're right, she says. It would be nice to have some aspects of nature in here for a change.

We ask her if she is speaking pragmatically now. We ask her if she had changed her whole mind about everything. We ask her if she would rather for the rest of her life just have ordinary windows to look out of, with ordinary eyes, at some boring old trees, or some shrubs in the yard, or an ordinary bird, than look at us, when we could move a certain way, and be the trees and the shrubs and the bird put together, if that was what she wanted us to be.

Don't be sentimental, she says. Don't be talking like cartoons from Walt Disney.

We say, we don't want to hurt you. We say, we'll expect that, now, right now, when we walk across this room, which we are just about ready to do, you will cover your eyes with both hands and not look at us.

After we're gone, will she wonder, how did they look when they walked by me? What steps were they doing that I missed? How were they holding their shoulders? How did they rotate their hips?

We tell her, dusk will come soon, and evening will come, and night will come, the same as always. Will you sit here alone in the dark and ask yourself, what steps were they doing that I missed out on?

We say, too bad you haven't got a blindfold in here to make it easier on your eyes not to look at us, and she says, oh, for crying out loud, and we say, do you have to get another new hip?

Not in the next half hour, she says. But eventually, I suppose that I will have to.

Please try teaching us a little faster. Please will you try to teach us faster?

Thank you very much for your concern, she says, and we bow to her, and she says, oh, now I will show you something new.

She goes out to the kitchen and we hear her in there banging around some cabinet doors.

She comes back with her arms full of shoe boxes. You can tell which hip is not her real one from how she walks. She walks like someone who doesn't have two legs that are matching in length. She walks like someone being tipped to one side.

She's got these shoe boxes and brings them over to us, and we don't know what to say.

She hands us the boxes. Look at this, she's giving us new shoes. We must have passed some kind of a test—and maybe it would feel like this in karate, when you get a new color of belt and everything gets important and then there's some kind of private ceremony.

But when we open the boxes of shoes, they're empty.

They're empty, Mrs. Kamsky, and she says, oh, go and get some others from my kitchen, I dropped some others on the floor, and we get the other ones, but they're as light as the air: they're all empty.

Give me some of those lids, she says, and we give her the lids and she walks away with them and comes back a while later with slits cut into them. Now put the lids back on the boxes, she says, and we do, and she says, now set the boxes on the floor, and we do, and she says, now squeeze your feet into those slits and wear the boxes, and we do.

But we say to her, no way are we walking around in these things, and she says, walking is not what you'll be doing, and now, when you show me all your fancy acrobatics, I hope you can think of a way to keep your shoes on.

These are not shoes, Mrs. Kamsky. These are boxes.

And she says, oh, but of course you would think so, you are clowns.

nibora

NIBORA WAS WALKING down Garfield Street one day and she came near the intersection. A lady said, "Is your name Robin Hazelton?"

"No," said Nibora.

"I beg your pardon," said the lady. She was at the bus stop. She sat on the bench. She was skinny. Her face had some wrinkles but not very many. She was polite. The walls of the bus stop were not made of glass. They were made of plexiglass. Everyone knows what this is. It's glass put together with plastic at a factory. The way that rain runs down it is different from the rain on real glass. It's the same with snow. Nothing would happen if someone kicked it.

"You know, I could have sworn that the name of the girl who's been looking into other people's windows on the street over there was Robin," said the lady. The street she pointed to was Garfield.

"I wouldn't know about that. My name is Nibora Kadoora," said Nibora.

"The little girl who's been looking into windows is in the second or third grade. She has brown curly hair. She has a small round face like a pumpkin."

The lady comes to the bus stop every day at 4:30. It is ten minutes after three. She should not be here at this time. There wasn't a bus down the valley into town until later. The lady lived in the town. The bus down the valley into town was at 4:35.

Nibora didn't want to be arrested. She did not believe that a cop would arrest a little girl. But she was always reminding herself to be careful. At the grocery store when she went down there, it was important to pick out the right people to blend in with, or pick the right time to run in and run out, at the shift change. But it wasn't that hard. She was small for her age. Sometimes when people asked her how old she was, she said, "I'm four. I'm not even old enough to go to kindergarten."

The lady wasn't supposed to be sitting on the bench in the shelter yet. This was the time of day when the bench belonged to Nibora. Everyone knew this. Maybe this was something the lady forgot about. The lady said, "The girl who's been looking in people's windows is very quiet, like a ghost."

"What color eyes did she have?"

"Dark," said the lady. "Dark and small and bright, like the eyes of a chipmunk."

"Does she have some spots on her face?"

The lady nodded yes. She said, "Sometimes when someone is looking somewhere, they can see something that they didn't think they would see."

"How many spots did she have?"

The lady held up one finger. She touched the tip of her finger to a few places on Nibora. She touched the side of Nibora's right eye. Four times, she touched Nibora's left cheek, and once on the right, and once on her nose, and twice on her chin. "Nine," said the lady.

Nibora said, "I heard from some kids I know that Robin Hazelton had chicken pox."

"I hope she's feeling better," said the lady.

Nibora didn't know what to do. "I have to go home now," she said.

"It was nice to talk to you," said the lady.

Nibora walked down the sidewalk. She didn't go far. Then she went back to the shelter. Sometimes she would go down the embankment at the back of house and get all the way through the woods behind the grocery store, but when she got to the store, she'd change her mind. She didn't know why. Everyone in the store would have looks on their faces like they were thinking about other things. No one in the store would look like, where they really wanted to be, was where they were. Everyone would look tired and sad. So there were two kinds of days when she went down there. There were stealing days, and there were days that were not right for stealing, not even one little bag of potato chips from the rack near the door.

She forgot when she first started going down there. It was a long time ago. What happened before, in the past, was not important, she felt.

It always felt good to run through the woods. It made her hungry. It was not really stealing if it's something you can eat, and you're just a little girl. But it's always a good idea to check over your shoulder when you're running away. The embankment was steep. It was hard to climb up when it was muddy. Nibora would take her shoes off and carry them with the laces in her teeth. She would need to use her hands as well as her feet on the embankment.

But Nibora couldn't lie down on the bench with the lady there, and look up. If you lie on the bench a certain way, you could see through the cracks in the roof and through the places in the trees where the branches did not join together like roofs of leaves. On a clear day like this one you could see all the way to where Pluto, the last planet, was.

Nibora sat down on the bench, but at the other end from the lady. Then she said, "Do you want me to tell you a good way to remember the planets? First there has to be Mercury, so you have to start with M. The last one is Pluto, so you have to end with a P."

"First M, last P, I think I've got it," said the lady. Then she said, "My name is Margaret Dunlap. You can call me Mrs. Dunlap."

"The bus doesn't come until 4:35," said Nibora.

"I can wait," said the lady.

"Did you get off work early today?"

"Sort of," said the lady. She pointed to a red house down the street.

"Is that your house?"

"No. That's where the Hazeltons live," said Nibora.

"I've heard they're nice people, and that Robin Hazelton's parents used to work in a bank, but now they have their own company."

"It's an investment company," said Nibora.

"Oh, I don't know anything about that at all," said the lady, and Nibora said, "Do you know what a factory is?"

"I do," said the lady.

"I heard from some people I know that Robin Hazelton's parents said an investment company is the same as a factory except, you don't have to have a real factory."

"I heard they moved their company into their garage," said the lady.

Nibora said, "Do you want to know about the planets?"

"Very much," said the lady, "but first, I wonder if you'd go over to the Hazeltons' for me and ask Robin Hazelton a question. You know, I was thinking about going over myself, and talking to Robin Hazelton's mom."

Nibora thought about this. "What's the question?"

"Oh, it's a secret."

"Is it about a window?"

"Does Robin want to talk about that?"

"She already did," said Nibora. "She told me. It wasn't even scary. She saw scarier stuff before on TV and scarier stuff in just commercials."

"Do you think that Robin Hazelton told anyone else what she saw in the window?"

"I'm her best friend," said Nibora. "I'm the only one she talks to. This is how you remember the planets. You say, my very educated mother just served us nice pizza."

"My very educated mother just served us nice pizza," said the lady.

"Mercury is first and Pluto is last," said Nibora.

"What goes in between?"

"Oh, everything in between doesn't matter very much," said Nibora, and the lady said, "What was the thing that wasn't scary?"

Nibora said, "Can you spell pharaoh? It doesn't have an f, you know." Then she said, "That was a clue."

"I was never good at spelling," said the lady.

"I'm great at it," said Nibora, and the lady said, "What was the thing?"

"I guess it was when a mummy got wrapped up in mummy clothes from a grave," said Nibora, because, this was what it was.

Some kids she knew went by on their bicycles. They looked surprised to see someone in the shelter, besides just Nibora Kadoora. A couple of cars went down the street. A cloud went by that looked like a snowplow, and then it was tangled all up, like a big white parachute, in the highest branches of some trees.

The lady said, "Would you like to be invited to come and visit the lady I work for?"

"I'm grounded," said Nibora. "I'm not supposed to go to any houses."

"We could go ask your mom."

"She would say no," said Nibora. "I kind of got into some trouble with some people. They don't live on this street anymore. One time I went there and I was kind of a little bit near their coffee table and it broke. It was kind of made of glass."

"The lady I work for doesn't have any coffee tables."

"Oh, I know," said Nibora. "She only has a couch."

"It's very comfortable. You could visit and sit there."

"No thank you," said Nibora. "Does the lady you work for know about the little girl?"

"Only I do," said the lady.

"Are you good or bad at secrets?"

"I'm very good. I'm excellent, in fact," said the lady.

"I'm perfect at it," said Nibora.

Then the lady said, "Do you think that Robin Hazelton will want to see some other things?"

"I'll have to ask her about that."

"Maybe she'd like to see something different from what she saw before. Maybe she'd like to see something a little nicer," said the lady.

"Maybe she wants to see something again that she already got used to."

"Maybe the lady I work for would be very unhappy if someone was looking in her window when she wanted to be private. Maybe she would not want to live on this street any-more."

"That wouldn't be a good thing," said Nibora.

"I would not have a job."

"You could get a job with the Hazeltons," said Nibora.

"I like the one I have," said the lady. "I'll tell you what I'm going to do. I am going to shut the window shades."

"Are you going to call the police?"

"No, I'm shutting the shades."

"Can I ask you a question?"

"You may."

"Can you leave them open one more time?"

The lady started thinking about that. Nibora thought that she would say no. But she said yes.

"I'll tell Robin."

"Good," said the lady, and Nibora went home. Mr. Kadoora was going into the office in the garage. He wanted to know who she was talking to at the bus stop and she said, "Somebody's maid from down the street," and he said, "Did you show her you're someone with good manners?"

"Yes," said Nibora. She went into the garage and said hello to Mrs. Kadoora. All the computers were on with just numbers so she couldn't play any games. She went into her house and ate some white cheese and nine saltine crackers. She watched a few TV shows and did her homework.

THE NEXT MORNING, there was a low blue sky. The white tulips in front of the lady's house were standing straight up, as if rods were in the ground instead of stems. The flowers were like big white cups, all white. Some other people in the neighborhood had tulips that were dark green, dark blue, dark red, and red-and-white striped, like candy canes, which were ugly and out of place. It was a long time away from the blooming of sunflowers, which would hang their heads and look sad.

There was a built-on addition that went out from the back of the lady's house and it wasn't like anyone else's. It went out from the back of the house like the long straight line of a T. It didn't have windows. The bedroom was on the side.

Nibora took off her book bag from her shoulders and put it down near the fence. She looked at the old weeping willows across the back of the yard. She always looked at the willows. She wondered if they were the oldest trees her eyes ever saw. The branches came down from the tops of the willows like green water from a fountain.

The first thing she saw in the room was the lady from the bus stop, only now she looked different. It was the different expression of someone who is working at their job, instead of sitting around and talking to you. There were some curtains on the window but they were open, same as always. One time when Nibora Kadoora was practically a baby, before she came to live in this neighborhood, she went with her mom to a hotel.

She remembers everything about it. But she pretends she forgot. It was a time when Nibora's mom cried a lot. She would talk on the phone in the hotel room and cry. Sometimes she would forget about dinner. Nibora and her mom stayed in the hotel for about a year. It was a time when Nibora's dad went somewhere else. She didn't know where. Just when Nibora thought she wasn't having a dad anymore, he came back. He came into the hotel room one day and she was happy to see him. She was mad, too, so she kicked him a few times, and he said, "Little girls who kick their dads will make their dads go away again," so she didn't, and then they came to live in this neighborhood.

In the hotel room was everything that went inside someone's house, but it was all put together in one room. This was what the bedroom of the lady was like.

It was a kitchen, a bedroom, and a living room. It had a bed and a microwave and a big wood cabinet like for keeping a TV inside and a little refrigerator and some chairs and a couch that was half of a couch, not the kind you can lie on. All these things were near each other so it was crowded. The lady from the bus stop had to move around sideways or she would always be bumping into things.

You had to know from looking in the window before about how there wasn't a TV in the cabinet. There were some shelves. The shelves were where they kept the mummy wrappings. Same with the little brown refrigerator.

There were two kinds of wrappings. One kind was cold from the little refrigerator and the other kind was from the cabinet and you had to put them into the microwave to heat them up. There wasn't any food in the refrigerator, just like in a hotel.

The bed didn't have any covers on it. It didn't have any pillows. It just had a white sheet. The covers and the pillows were on a chair. It was time for the lady to wrap the mummy. This was her job.

So then the mummy lay on the bed. All the wrappings were on. The wrappings on the mummy's face didn't have any air holes like you're supposed to have for breathing. The mummy was dead, again. Nibora didn't know how you could do this.

The mummy would be dead and then a prince would come in and he would walk around in a sideways way, not bumping into things. Just when you would think the mummy would always be dead, forever, she would come back to life. She would lift up her head and some wrappings would fall off her face and she would open her eyes and she would look at the prince. Then it would be time to take off all the wrappings. It wasn't always the same prince. There were different kinds. But they all were princes.

Nibora watched how the mummy got wrapped and she was afraid that it would be different this time because of talking to the lady at the bus stop. But it was the same as every day. And Nibora watched the prince come in. He didn't have many clothes on, just shorts. But this was okay because, he was a prince. And then it was time for the mummy to not be dead, and that was the way it always went, today was no different.

Nibora picked up her book bag and there was some mud on it and she brushed it away. When Nibora was in school and things weren't going very well, she put her head down on her desk and she would think about what the princes looked like. It was strange when a boy didn't have a shirt on. You would think they would not look like a girl. But they do. They even have little nipples.

One day Nibora's teacher said, "You little daydreamer, what are you always dreaming about?"

"A prince," said Nibora, and her teacher said, "Like in *Cinderella?*"

"No," said Nibora.

"Like in *Sleeping Beauty?*"

"No, a real prince," said Nibora.

But her teacher didn't think she was telling the truth. One time, Nibora was talking to her mom and she said to her, "Why do boys have nipples?" "I don't know," said Nibora's mom. So it would have to be a mystery.

After that, the shade of the bedroom window was always pulled down. But pretty soon after that, Nibora found out that the princes were boy ballerinas. She kind of really knew that all along. There were four of them, and then there was a new one, and there were five.

Sometimes she wondered if she should explain to the boy ballerinas that Nibora was really a Robin spelled backward, and Kadoora was a name she made up. Sometimes it would seem to be important, and sometimes she would say to herself, "Oh, let them think whatever they want to."

NOW THIS IS WHAT Nibora is doing. At 4:45, when the bus had gone down into town, Nibora comes to the back of the built-on addition.

The lady at the piano is round like a hen in a storybook. She looks over her shoulder at Nibora. But if she notices that Nibora is in the doorway, she doesn't show it, the same as if she were blind.

It's just like when she was in her own bed with all her wrappings on. It's all the same lady. When she sits on the bench at the piano with her feet in the front and her back to the piano keys, this is what she is: she is queen of the boy ballerinas. When she turns around again and plays the piano, she isn't the queen anymore, she's a piano player. This is how it works.

"You can come in. Come on, she doesn't eat children," say the boy ballerinas. Nibora doesn't think they're making fun of her in an unfriendly way. They're explaining that, the lady at the piano is not a witch, which Nibora knew already: she's not stupid.

The door at the back, where the willow trees are, is open a little to let in air. The air going into the built-on addition is yellow with some very light green mixed in, from the willow leaves. Inside it always gets hot. You can't be opening windows if there aren't any windows. There are walls, a railing, and mirrors on the wall that had the railing. It's a wall of silver mirrors.

Nibora Kadoora doesn't want to go inside. She is the kind of person who would rather look at things from outside in.

She has something for the boy ballerinas. In the doorway, she opens her pack and takes out Milky Ways, Reese's Peanut Butter Cups, and those expensive bars from foreign countries, the kind that don't have nuts or caramel, just chocolate. You would think that the aisle of the grocery store with the foreign food would be the one the store detectives would watch the most, but they don't.

Nibora hands out candy to the boys. They come to the back door to get some air, in a pause before they start dancing again.

It feels to Nibora that this is like Halloween, a reverse Halloween. It's funny to have the ones dressed up in costumes be the ones inside, and then, the one outside the door is the one with all the treats.

The boy ballerinas say, "You should let us give you money for bringing us lunch," and Nibora says, "It's not lunch, it's candy," and the boys say, "No, really, it's our lunch," and Nibora says, "It's candy."

Nibora never speaks to the lady. One time, Nibora asked a boy, "Is she blind?"

The boy said, "Oh, we would never get that lucky," and Nibora got the feeling he was joking.

There's no gate in the fence at the back behind the willows, but it takes Nibora less than one second to climb over it.

The lady is playing the piano. You can hear it all the way down the block, through the shiny green air, the same song over and over, through the grass and the flower beds and the trees, along the sidewalk, past the bus stop, dee dee dee dah dah, dah dah dah dah dee, dee dee dee, dee dee dee, dah dah.

Nibora has the feeling that the notes the lady is playing are going home with her. Nibora thinks that the lady is *talking* to her with her piano, which does not make sense, when all that the lady was ever doing, all along, was playing for the boy ballerinas, not for Nibora. The lady did not give a hint to Nibora that she could see her, not at all.

mr. friedrich

THERE USED TO BE the four of us, me, Davey Peete, this kid named Eddie Mastromatteo, and Shaun Mullins. Me and Eddie Mastromatteo and Davey were normal and Shaun was normal too but he had this fag brother that went off to New York City to be a fag ballerina wearing makeup like a girl and shaving his legs. There's Lady Bics all over the bathroom at his house when his brother comes home and they don't have a sister and their mother is not the type. Also you go over there and there's about fourteen pictures of Shaun's brother hanging all over the walls in big gold frames with other fags like it's no big deal, like he's a movie star, they just accept it.

It's understandable when it comes to this kind of thing, with his family background, how Shaun gets it into his head that someone needs to be defending our teacher Mr. Bird. And the someone has got to be him.

For a while, it was going along okay like this. "Lay off Bird you guys," is how far it went from Shaun until the stuff came down about Bird getting into recruitment techniques for signing up new kids to be fags. Up to that point me and Eddie Mastromatteo and Davey, we could have tolerated it.

Like the injunction said, in civil rights, you can't hold it against a teacher for being a fag and they can't get fired by the school board, long as they didn't walk in here inflicting their sex on you. They had to keep quiet about it. They had to give you stuff to read that was normal. If there's a bed in some book, and two people are in it, they have to be different sexes. Plus, kids walking into classrooms with disposable rubber gloves on like some kids kept in their lockers, they had to have

71

a reason for the gloves, instead of the one where, their teacher is a fag. Do this anymore, you can get stopped in the hall. We have this new security force. You get hit with a three-day detention. They put it in the computer where, they keep track, it adds up, and all of a sudden you're getting this letter in the mail that you won't get to graduate with your own class.

Bird never mentioned it when he's handing out some kind of form in his class or some books, and kids put on rubber gloves. He'd be like, he didn't notice. You could walk around naked, especially the girls, he wouldn't know. He'd be bumming out anyway on something else.

Bird is like nobody else anybody ever knew. He is about fifty or sixty. He's got this big bald head, almost all the way bald. He's got this face like, you look at him, you're going, oh, evolution. You understand evolution. It's like an ape was his uncle. *The Legend of Sleepy Hollow* is his favorite thing to read. He read it to us one day in reading skills class, and he must of felt like he was looking in a mirror. Ichabod Crane, it looks just like him, except Bird's not skinny. All fags are gourmet cooks and Bird looks like he eats fancy dinners, like every night. He never works out, either.

Only about half of Bird's weirdness is from homosexuality. The rest is personal. It's wired in his brain cells. He's a total depressive, which is strange to deal with in someone that isn't a history teacher. With history teachers you expect it, it's an occupational hazard. They know about stuff from before, it's all they ever think about, and every single word of it is bad.

Me and Shaun and Eddie Mastromatteo and Davey got Bird this year for homeroom and also for reading skills. Bird's so loaded down with depression that, you go into homeroom, he's supposed to be acting teacherly. He's supposed to be telling you how sixth period Tuesday got changed to fourth, or they're closing the pool because they're cleaning it or something. We never know anything that goes on.

Bird'll sit there looking at the wall. We'll go, Mr. Bird, take attendance before the bell rings, and he'll look at us and go, are you here? We go, yeah, everybody's here, write it down. Then somebody has to find a pen and do it for him. The quietest homeroom there ever was in our school is our homeroom, like we have to be quiet so we know he's still sitting there breathing.

Then there was this one day, first period. Somebody was in our reading class the night before, some night school thing, some ladies' poetry group. They didn't erase the board. We knew Bird didn't write the stuff on the board because he walked in there with us from homeroom.

"I'll be damned," said Bird. This look came over him. His face like lit up. It was like he was this lightbulb in a lamp and somebody had put a blanket on top of it and they just pulled it off and pulled off the lampshade, too. It made us nervous. Or we were saying, how come he never looks like this when it's because of us? So we had these negative things going on at the beginning.

It was some poem in perfect lady penmanship writing. I never looked at it in terms of what the words were. When Bird wrote on the board he'd go off in all these slants, like in first grade, he never learned to handle straight lines. He'd write on the board like he was blind.

The other thing that factors in here is how this was around the middle of autumn. It was between Halloween and Thanksgiving. And this was a tricky time of year for the Mullins family because it was getting near the time for *The Nutcracker*.

Shaun's brother is some primo hotshot in it. Comes home this time of year so he can have everybody over there fussing with him. He eats steak, that's all, even for breakfast, and he lies around sleeping all day and goes out to some faggot he knows to get his body rubbed. Then the whole family, they take the train to New York City and go see him. Every year it goes on like this. If we say to Shaun, you can stay at my house in case you want to skip this thing, he looks at us like, this guy is my *brother*. Shaun's brother was on his way home to get ready for *The Nutcracker* on the morning we walked into our reading skills room and Mr. Bird saw the poem on the board.

A couple of girls and a couple of kids who are out of it on a regular basis sat down in the desks like nothing dangerous was going on. They took out their books. "We're on the part where so-and-so is just about ready to blah, blah, blah, Mr. Bird," says a girl. She was keeping our place overnight in what Bird was making us read. Otherwise Bird would get up there and go into this retreat, and then he looks at you, like he just woke up. He'd say, "Mr. Mullins, did we read this section yesterday?" Or he'd say, to me, "Mr. Friedrich, please describe what took place so far without using the words 'I forget.'" If Shaun or me or whoever he called on doesn't know the answer, or you answer it wrong, this new cloud of gloom coming in would totally bypass Mr. Bird. The ones that would get all sucked up in it would be us. So this girl was keeping our place. "We're on page so-and-so, Mr. Bird," she says, but Bird's pointing to the board. "Everybody copy this down, and then we'll talk about it."

There's this general thing of, he's kidding. Kids start putting up some resistance, same as always, like trying to figure out how far you can go with Bird without him flicking up his thumb in the air and leaning it sideways in the direction of the door, and you're out. Try arguing about it, Bird just says, "So get a lawyer." As soon as you step out the door of a classroom into the hall before the period's over, the security forces are

out there, and you're nailed with automatic add-it-up detention.

Some girls are going, no way are we writing down any
poem that wasn't even for us. Or, I didn't bring anything to
write with. Or, this isn't on the lesson plan, like this was
something Bird would have. Some of the kids that are inex-
perienced with Bird, they're putting their heads down and
making throw up noises, but me and Eddie Mastromatteo are
saying, "Please, Mr. Bird, we want to see what happens in
what we're reading, we're real excited about it. We do this
like we're playing Eddie Haskell on the old black-and-white
Beaver show. Lots of times, with Bird, this really works. He
wouldn't get it. Somebody told me once that like all faggots
everywhere, Bird doesn't own a TV, and I believe it.

"People," goes Bird. "Let's get to it."

Shaun and Davey are standing up. They're over by the
board. Bird goes, "Mr. Mullins and Mr. Peete, if you would
take your seats and follow my directions, I predict that the
next forty minutes will go by for you a little more tolerably
than if you don't," and some girl says, "Do we have to copy
this dumb thing down like it is or can we put it all together
in a paragraph," and Bird says, "You have to do it like it is,"
and the girl says, "I only have half a piece of paper," and Bird
says, "It'll fit."

Some kids say Davey's this kind of kid where, he's autistic, like, "Davey Peete's totally autistic." He's not autistic. He
can make up his mind. He is *focused*. He's got this talent for
it. He could get himself going on this wavelength or something.

Davey's whole family is in the construction business. He's
smaller than Shaun, just like everyone else. But on account of
his genes, he always had some extra stuff going on, like he
was born with some extra muscles, and his hands are real

strong, too. Some day like we used to always say to each other, like back in the days when it still was the four of us, Steve-Davey-Shaun-Eddie, let's go to some town somewhere where nobody knows us, and set up Davey to Indian wrestle some kids, or even some grown-ups, and get some bets up.

Davey and Shaun are still standing up near the board. Bird thinks the one he has to pay attention to the most is Shaun, not Davey, so he says, "Mr. Mullins, I believe I had invited you to sit down," and he doesn't see what Davey's face is like when Davey's saying to Shaun, "Hand me that eraser." Davey looks like he's saying to himself, "I am *edgy.*"

Shaun's got this blackboard eraser in his hands. It's the only eraser. He holds it behind his back. Maybe if Davey hadn't started getting himself on this certain track, he would of settled down, satisfied that he wasn't getting thrown to the security forces.

How he got the poem off the board so fast, I don't know, he had these really good reflexes. He used both his shirt-sleeves. He had this Adidas sweatshirt on, a dark blue one. He had it smeared all over with chalk dust.

The lines on the board are like when a plane's in the sky doing skywriting, and the wind blows all wrong. Eddie M. says, "Way to go, Davey," and Davey says, "Injunction said no one's putting fag stuff in our face. We get to tell the school board when he's violating the injunction," and some girl says, "Davey, you're totally autistic, and you are also a jerk," and Bird says to the girl, "Put a lid on that, Michelle," and Davey says, like he's the one teaching the class, "This thing on the board was what you call a subliminal technique and it's a secret recruitment thing for more fags," which is not what Shaun Mullins feels like hearing. Bird's like, "Shaun, sit *down.*"

And one thing starts leading to another, and Bird's not quick, in this way that teachers learn in school or something, like when a fight's breaking out, you have to put yourself in the middle, which Bird does, but he's not in time. Eddie M. had just got done saying to me, "What did it say?"

And I told him, I don't know how come exactly, except how, I kind of got caught up in this, and there was definitely some tension going on, "I think it was a poem about two queers, and he was going to make us memorize it," and this other kid who was trying to get in good with me and Davey and Shaun and Eddie M., he says, "They were roses," so this set off Eddie M., and he says, to me, "Let's go help out Davey."

When it came to the poem on the board, everyone forgot that it was already there when we first went in.

So Shaun was up there telling Davey to lay off fags, and Bird finally got around to seeing this was serious and he says, "Time out here, guys. Mr. Mullins and Mr. Peete, time *out.*" And then a couple more things got said in some louder voices and we could hear the security forces coming toward us from down the hall, and we didn't think Bird would take so long in getting in the middle. If Bird was in the middle quicker, maybe it wouldn't of gotten out of hand. Even in the worst way Davey could get, like when he'd lose it, really lose it, he would know enough to hold back from laying into a teacher, especially when the teacher was Bird, who anyway was protected special by the injunction, like on the federal endangered list, like sea cows or something, or seals.

There is this certain kind of break-out fight where, it can turn kind of vicious really early. You're in a hurry, you dispense with the preliminaries. Some kids took Shaun's side, plus all the girls except a couple that moved away to the back of the room and said, "We're immune from Bird recruiting us on account of being girls."

Davey broke Shaun's knee. He gave this jump in the air and kicked Shaun's kneecap. He only had on his Nikes. No one knew before he could kick like that, using your foot like it's a hammer.

Everyone's going, Shaun's on the floor, Shaun's on the floor. And the security forces are coming in, and Bird's got this look on his face like, you had to look away from him immediately.

It wasn't a riot like everyone starting saying about it. Riots need to take a little longer and more people would need to have injuries besides Shaun, and some stuff would need to be trashed, which didn't happen.

A couple days after, I'm walking home from school. No one's around, it's this cold day, it's getting ready to snow. I'm not thinking about fags or fights. I'm not thinking about *anything,* and the next thing I know, I'm crossing the street to my house and this car, this convertible with the top up, this little red car, a Corvette, I think it was, but an old one, with a black convertible top, it shoots out of nowhere and comes up between me and the curb. It stops one inch away from me, a perfect dead stop, without screeching any brakes, which is something I noticed. Shaun's brother is at the wheel, and he says, "How's it going, Friedrich."

"Pretty good."

"School going okay?"

"School's great."

Things are real quiet about how come there was a fight like that in Bird's room. The way we were looking at it was, me and Eddie M. and a few other kids who got involved took a one-day suspension and so did Davey, like we all were in it together, and we would call it an accident. We were supposed to be under review from the school board but Bird wasn't saying anything except, "I think that they were rebelling against poetry." He was passing it off as some normal hormonal thing and kids were all shutting up too, like Shaun's knee got broken for a bunch of flowery words. When Davey had kicked Shaun, he had aimed. I kept seeing him aiming.

Shaun's brother says, "Want a ride to the hospital to see my brother?"

I go, in this serious way, "Maybe I'll go later. I got to do some homework."

"Maybe you could get in the car." And just then, over at my house, my mom shows up in the doorway. She sees who's in the car and she's like, she's ready to run out and ask him for his autograph. She's hanging out the door yelling. "Oh, it's Nutcracker time already! Oh, it's great to see you!"

"It's good to see you too, Mrs. Friedrich. I'm giving your son a ride to see my brother!"

"That's so nice of you! If your parents don't buy you enough steak, come over here! You're so invited!"

He is looking at my mom all movie star smiley and he's looking at me, the same time, completely grim. In front of my mom I act like getting picked up on the sidewalk by Shaun's brother is okay and I don't let on that basically I'm in the situation of someone that's being kidnapped or taken as a hostage, which would not've done me any good, even if she believed me, because she'd call up my dad and freak out at him and go, "Our son gets in weird situations because you suck as a parent and you divorced me."

I get in the car with Shaun's brother. He throws the car into gear and does a three-point turn in one short half of a loop without leaving any rubber, and we could probably go like ninety miles an hour in this thing, and this car is like *small.*

"Nice car," I say, and he's like, "It's not mine."

"Bet you could go zero to eighty no sweat when we get out on the highway."

He says, "Any idiot can open up. It's much more interesting to me to keep stuff like this under control." We go thirty like some old lady.

Shaun's brother is about nineteen. I remember how one time in the winter, when we were just kids, me and Eddie M. and Davey were over at Shaun's house with Shaun and his dad, and his dad was building us this fort out of ice blocks, like he was always doing this type of thing on account of Shaun's brother getting all the attention. He was always in these recitals. Shaun didn't care, Shaun was glad that if someone had to be a ballerina in his family, it didn't have to be him. We're out there in these snowmobile suits we had building this fort and I looked over in their driveway and there was Shaun's brother wearing white boxer shorts, that was all. His skin was even whiter. He was standing by their family's car in the driveway like that, barefoot. Snow came up around his ankles. He wasn't shivering, he wasn't doing anything but standing there, for about five minutes. He tipped back his face like he was working on a tan. He held out his arms like he's a high-platform diver in the Olympics, swung them down, held them up. He did that a couple of times like it wasn't about ten below zero. Then Shaun's dad looks up from this corner of the fort he was fixing, and yells across the yard, "That's five, son, time's up," and Shaun says to his brother, "Looking good," and Shaun's brother's like, "Thanks, guys." He turned around and went into their house. A little while later we could hear this piano music coming out of the windows. It was like this tinkle tinkle tinkle kind of thing, but it felt okay to be hearing it. If I heard it again I would think of how the sunlight was all white like that shining down on our ice blocks, and how it felt to be wearing our suits, like we were out on the moon or something, and Shaun's brother could stand there practically naked and not shiver. It was weird seeing footprints of someone's bare feet in the snow.

We get to the hospital where Shaun's brother pulls up in front into this parking space that says, "Reserved for Chief of Orthopedics." I know from being here before and seeing people in here or getting x-rays, the hospital's got its own meter maids, which maybe Shaun's brother forgot about, from being away, so I mention it, and he says, "The doctor whose spot this is said we could use it. Get out of the car." If the top was down I could've jumped it.

Over at the entrance there's some hospital stuff going on, there's people in wheelchairs getting wheeled and looking really depressed, there's people coming and going. Then over at the side of the door, inside the lobby, there's three people. Shaun's brother waves to them. They're sitting on a couch in there. As soon as they see us they get up. It's not like Shaun's brother's crowding me or anything, like he's handcuffed to me, but he's kind of got me covered.

Two of these people are these two older ladies, one kind of fat and the other one kind of thinner, and kind of pinched-up in her face or something, and the other one's Bird.

I'm like, "Hey, Mr. Bird," and he looks at me like this is the first time he ever saw me.

I never saw Bird outside of school. It kind of throws me. He looks older. He looks like this big old middle-aged fag, like there's even less hair on his head than in school, and there's three or four gray hairs in the back and the rest is total baldness, and he's got about nineteen layers of clothes on except nothing on his head, and he's wearing this big gray wool coat like he just got off a boat here from Russia or something, only, he doesn't look Russian, he looks American. It's like he's not this teacher I always saw. He's like this big bald eagle or something, combined with being faggoty. I'm thinking, I never should've got into that car.

Shaun's brother hands over the car keys to the fatter lady and she goes, "Is this the one who kicked him?" And the skinny one says, "Oh, I hope not." Bird looks at me for this really long time out the sides of his eyes and he goes, "This one's Friedrich."

Shaun's brother says, "We've already got the one who kicked him upstairs. I thought you wanted me to get them all."

The thinner one says, "She changed her mind."

"Oh, you can send this one back," says the fatter one and Shaun's brother says to me, "Have you got money for a taxi?" I say, yeah, my mom can pay when I get there, and then I say, "I thought I was seeing Shaun."

"He's not here. He went home. But his room was paid up for the day so we're borrowing it," says Shaun's brother, like this is some kind of hotel, not a hospital.

Everyone but me went walking down the hall to the elevator and these nurses were going by and they stop, and they're making a commotion like, oh, look who's here.

The fatter lady acts like she's getting kissed. I'm thinking, the fat one was probably a patient here or something but then it didn't feel like that. And a couple secretaries come out of these little offices and go, oh, oh, and the fatter lady's like, if she was wearing some better clothes, she'd be the queen of England's mother. That's what it looks like, like when English stuff is on TV, and Mr. Bird's holding the elevator and Shaun's brother is like, when he looks at this lady, he looks just like Bird when Bird saw the poem on the blackboard, and the thinner one, like, this isn't some kind of fag thing only, the thinner one was just the same.

The fatter one's in the middle of all this attention like it's Hollywood and she's wearing this outfit my mom would wear when she was going to court again to get the judge to go after my dad on his child support, like total dump city, with this old brown tweed coat and a kerchief around her head, and six-dollar shoes from Bradlees.

Then I'm back outside, and I'm looking up at the windows, and I'm thinking, what are they doing up there to Davey Peete? But that's not what I kept thinking about. I kept thinking about the hospital lobby when I got there and how Bird was there and how he looked at me out the sides of his eyes. Then he had looked away like I wasn't there. It was weird when he said, "This one's Friedrich." I had noticed what his voice was like. It wasn't that he sounded disappointed. "This one's Friedrich." He sounded like someone reading my name off a list or something, like totally not knowing me, but that was minor compared to the rest of it. It was like, where he always used to say "Mister," he left it out, and it wasn't like I got the feeling it was accidental, or, he talked to you different in public, from how he talked to you in school. No one else had a teacher that called you "Mister" like the nineteenth century.

As soon as I heard him leave it out I tried to remember how I never had liked it when Bird called me "Mr. Friedrich," like I was my dad, but I must've gotten used to it. I was thinking, "I'm not bumming out because of Bird leaving off the Mister," but there was this blank in front of "Friedrich" that you had to pay attention to, like you'd notice it if you're walking along somewhere and your feet go into a hole.

I went home. Eddie M. called me up and says, "I don't want to talk about this but I'm transferring to Catholic school like, tomorrow."

Maybe I should've gone over to Shaun's that same day but I didn't. Maybe I should've been surprised when I found out how this was the day when Davey Peete started turning into a ballerina, but I wasn't. It wasn't like they gave him any choice.

a stolen room

SHE WANTED TO LEAVE the world. There had been for her a succession of disappointments. I do not believe that I was one of them.

She was not sentimental. She was a pragmatist. Did I ever see her dance? She already had stopped, when I met her. Did I ever see her dance in a room that was mine, when no one was in there, except myself and Irene Kamsky?

Didn't have to see her dance to know what she looked like when she danced.

She put everything of her own into storage, I don't know where. I have no idea where her things are. It was strictly a matter between us of, you want to go somewhere else? Go. You want to leave the world? I'm staying in it.

Now she is never alone. Call her up, not that often, voices in the background, much background noise all the time, not exactly a state of tranquility. Call her up Christmas, call her up Easter, call her up for her birthday, it's hard to get through. Lives out there like Mother Goose.

You want money for an addition on your house? I will give you the money for your addition.

You want money for a hip? I will give you the money for a hip.

You want money for a nursemaid? I will give you the money for a nursemaid.

You want two thousand dollars for mirrors? I will give you two thousand for mirrors.

You want me to come out there and see you? Don't ask for the moon. Goodnight, Irene, goodnight, Irene, I'll see you instead in my dreams. Don't get me going. She took my living room. I don't mean that, after she left me, I couldn't sit and listen to my stereo because the room for me without her was spoiled. The room for me without her was an empty room. Came home one afternoon, had to walk out and walk in again to believe it.

Shouldn't have bothered asking questions. Doorman says, Been here all day. If someone was robbing you, I'd of seen it. Guy who's been painting the hallways. Was up that day on my floor. Says, Nobody went by me with any furniture. Press him on this. Short chubby middle-aged lady? Walks around like she needs a new hip? Maybe had a couple of guys with her? Big, young, self-centered guys? Athletic types? Maybe wearing some really tight clothes? Waltzing down the hall with my sofa? Painter says, I saw nothing. What about a guy around forty, big guy almost all the way bald, long overcoat? Painter says, I look brain dead to you, mister, or what.

Never asked anymore. Windows and floor of the living room, all bare, nothing on the floor but dust balls, and some dark green bits of woolly lint, that were always being shed by my rug. She took the curtains, the shades, the curtain rods, the screws. Puncture marks on the corners at the top of the sills look like bite marks in the wood. She took the stereo, everything. My sofa. My rug. Didn't have any pictures in there. This was up on the twenty-second floor. Didn't need any pictures. Had windows. Everything else in the place, all intact. It was only my living room. She only took that one room. Wasn't like she emptied me out. Nothing was in there but a big white sofa, curtains on rods, a three thousand dollar hi fi, my green rug, the windows, myself, Irene Kamsky, light, music, air.

a white hole

WE HAD THIS PERFORMANCE in Hartford, no big deal. We were fillers. Somebody called up Mrs. Kamsky at the last minute. It was only a single night. We were supposed to head straight back. But then we stayed around the theater on our own, not doing anything, just standing around outside the door and watching what it looked like when it got emptier and emptier and then they shut off the lights.

It got to be too late for the train we were supposed to take back, and we called up Mrs. Kamsky collect and asked her, could we check into some hotel or something, we're kind of stranded here, and she said, "There's not enough money, take the bus." When it comes to our parents, we didn't feel like telling anyone where we were going. They think we're sleeping over at each other's houses like little kids.

We didn't have enough cash for the bus tickets so we called up again and Mrs. Kamsky put it on her credit card and then we had to get back on the phone with her at the ticket counter.

"Put those boys back on the phone, please," and the ticket agent keeps watching our faces like we're trying to rob her. There were all these people, all around, hanging around, and these tiny television sets in the waiting area. You put in some quarters and watch TV on about two inches of screen, which is depressing. "Everybody gets disappointed when they go out on their own, their first time," Mrs. Kamsky said, and we said, "We're not disappointed, it went great," and she said, "Everyone always lies about it, too."

We had about an hour to wait. There was a McDonald's so we went over there. We ordered and took the food outside and ate standing up in the parking lot. Inside was too depressing to eat in.

We balled up the trash and went over to a trash barrel near the back of the parking lot. We started walking away, but something had moved against the barrel. It sounded too big to be a rat, which was the first thing we thought of. It was a dog.

It was crouched at the side of the barrel. It was a three- or four-year-old bitch, an old mutty thing, with matted fur, and it was small, like a sheltie mixed with a hound. Its eyes were a dull shade of yellow. Its fur looked damp, and it was filthy. Its red teats hung low to the ground. It must have whelped like five or six days ago. There were some trees behind McDonald's and then an auto body shop with broken windows that looked like it had been closed a long time. Probably the dog's litter was over there, but we couldn't hear any yelping or anything.

The dog backed away from us. It smelled us before it saw us. We saw the way the fur bristled. Its legs were as thin as popsicle sticks. It leaned against the barrel like it couldn't stand up much longer on its own. "Wait here," we said.

We took out our wallets and got in line and got the same girl who had just waited on us. We ordered double burgers with nothing on them, to go. The girl was about a sophomore or a junior. She had blond hair that looked like she started putting hair dye in it when she was about nine. "You want fries?" she said. She didn't recognize us from not even five minutes ago, and it wasn't like the place was jumping or anything. We wanted the burgers without the bread, but couldn't think of a way to explain this.

When we got back to the trash barrel the dog was gone. We took out the burgers and unwrapped them and threw the paper and cardboard away. We stood there for a while. If the dog was still around somewhere, it would catch the smell.

Some people getting into their cars, and some people in line for the drive-up window, looked at us standing there with these burgers in our hands. We had all of our stuff in backpacks so we looked normal. Back in the dressing room, we took a really long time getting rid of the fact that we had makeup on. The dressing room was nothing special. It looked like something straight out of a YMCA built about a hundred years ago. But the way we looked, we didn't have to freak out about personal safety on the basis of, we're in a strange city late at night and we're these dancers.

Were we supposed to peel the bread off the burgers too? Then we heard it. It had moved over to the side of the parking lot. There weren't any cars over there. It was standing on the curb in front of the kind of bushes that all McDonald's always have. It let out a low, yowling sound, like it needed to stretch out its jaws. Some saliva came out of its mouth.

Its two back legs were shaking like something in an earthquake. "Hey," we said. "We know how you feel."

We got down and put the burgers on the ground, on the blacktop of the curb. Nothing happened. The dog just kept looking at us with slitted eyes. It paid no attention to the food, but some more saliva was on its muzzle.

"We have to get on a bus," we said to the dog.

We started walking across the parking lot toward the bus station. We looked over our shoulders. The dog had waited until we were just far enough away from it to not be able to kick it. It had measured the distance the same as if it had thrown out a measuring tape, like, this is how long a leg is, and this is exactly how many inches of air a human would need to swing up the right momentum.

Then it flung itself at the burgers so fast its hind legs skidded up, and it almost fell over frontward. We watched the way its neck tipped back as it swallowed.

We were just about to cross the street back over to the bus station when the dog came loping up to us with its long red teats all jiggling.

"Hey," we said. "Good dog." It nosed up to us. We touched the glossy patch between its eyes. We rubbed the dog's head with our knuckles. We liked what it felt like to touch something that was real. It was only just one simple thing: an old stray beat-up dog with puppies somewhere. It couldn't ever pretend to be anything it wasn't.

The dog butted its head against our hands and licked our fingers. We couldn't figure out if it was thanking us for the meal, or if it was sniffing around for more food.

"Go on, git," we said. We put our hands in our jacket pockets. We turned away from the dog and crossed the street. Maybe we had expected it to try to follow us. At the door of the bus station we were all set to turn around and explain to the dog why it couldn't come home with us. We just had this feeling it was with us, like, it seemed to be really important. What difference should it make if the stupid dog was thanking us, or asking us for more food? It was a dog. It didn't follow us one inch. Why should it? It wasn't like, this was Old Yeller or something, or some other famous story about a great, faithful animal that sticks with you no matter what.

We got a seat to ourselves on the bus. We spread out. We put our packs on the next seat beside us. When people got on we looked at their faces. We kept wondering if any of the passengers were in the audience. There was a married couple of about sixty or something with good clothes on. They sat up in their seat with their backs straight. We took off our jackets and bunched them up against the windows. We leaned over and made like we were sleeping.

When we passed by streetlights or big lit-up signs we got the feeling that the married couple was looking at us. Like maybe they thought they recognized us.

We didn't mind it. We didn't know that when you're out there, you wouldn't be able to see the audience.

Probably they had gone to a restaurant for dinner, or they were visiting their relatives. It wasn't that big of a deal. You're like, out there, and you don't even know where the edge of the stage is. The lights are like this huge wide hole, like brighter than a white-out in a snowstorm, when the sun is at the back of the snow, and you feel like your eyelids are scorched off.

It's like something went wrong with the *air*. Like, this is what it must feel like if you're an astronaut in outer space, and the whole front side of your ship just all of a sudden blew away on you, and you're like, they didn't tell me this might happen. The place you're crash-landing to is a star, like you're heading straight away for the corona of the sun, or something.

When we were standing around outside the theater afterward, two people walked by, talking about the orchestra. "The orchestra was so sloppy with the adagio," said a woman to a man, and the man said, "That was because the violinists wore their mittens again tonight." "Well, it was cold in there," said the woman. And we were like, "It was cold? They had an orchestra?"

It wasn't like we were doing this immature thing and expecting something great.

We're like, "We'll be careful, we'll be careful," when about eighteen people afterward kept telling us not to walk around by ourselves, and just get into a cab and go straight to the train and make sure to get off all the makeup, like we wouldn't have known this.

All along when we were out there, there was this hot white hole, and that was all, the whole universe turned into this hole. We felt better about things because the dog ate the hamburgers, even though it had only lasted for one minute.

sissy

I HAD HEARD the strange news that my neighbor on Garfield Street was in the Federal Witness Protection Program, so I called my brother and demanded that he tell me what he knew. My brother has a small but successful computer consultancy business and of his clients, there is the FBI, and he socializes all the time with people who are agents. And he knows all the policemen here. When it comes to the station, he's got all their computers wired, he's down there all the time, he knows all the policemen in the valley.

I was as shocked by the news as anyone else. I did not know my neighbor. I had hardly ever spoken to her. She had only been living here for three or four months. But I decided that, unless she had committed, or had been an accomplice to, a crime that was purely unforgivable, I'd be perfectly happy to help keep her secret from the outside world, and I was sure that the rest of our neighbors felt the same.

Our neighbor would not have known this about me, but I was prepared to stick by her. I had wanted her to look at me as a source of trustfulness, as if our neighbors were a tribe she had stumbled upon, like an old-fashioned archaeologist in a jungle: when everyone else went running for their bows and poisoned arrows, I'd defend her. It must have been lonely for her. "Oh, she's in Witness Protection. That's why she's so mysterious, and that's why she never talks to anyone," were the things that people were saying.

My brother was very discouraging. He told me that I was the fourteenth or fifteenth person who had called him about this, and it just went to show you what people can be like when their lives are ruled by boredom and television. He didn't know how the rumor got started, and neither did any of his friends, but that's all it was, a rumor. He was absolutely sure. Frankly he was getting sick of it. Did I know how this whole dumb thing got started? I said that I did not; I said, oh, everyone is talking about it, but in fact, I had heard about it first from a woman named Ethel Bascomb, our librarian. Last winter, a portion of a plaster wall in the children's room had collapsed (it had happened at night, and no one was injured). Ethel had covered up the hole with posters. She'd been sweeping white dust till she was ready to scream, and finally, just last week, someone came through with some money to get it fixed, and the guys who came to fix it were the Peetes, of Peetes' Construction, who were taking a break from the job which they'd happened to be on, which was building an addition at the back of Mrs. Kamsky's gray house.

Jimmy Peete, twenty years old, must be thought of as the originator. But it wasn't Jimmy's fault that something starting out as a personal speculation should have taken on legs of its own. All he'd actually ever said (this came out later) was something along the lines of, "This lady's house we've been working on, she hasn't got anything personal in there, and it kind of reminds me of like, is this lady in the Witness Protection Program?"

Had he only said this to one or two people, the rumor would never have expanded the way it did. But Jimmy Peete was a well-known sociable person, and so were all the members of his family. It's not a good sign in a builder that they go around talking about the houses and the lives of the people who are clients of theirs, but this was different. Neither Jimmy Peete nor his relatives had ever said anything with a grain of concrete truth about Mrs. Kamsky, beyond their

own opinion. "It *looks* like she's in Witness Protection," was
what they said, and, "it *reminded* me."

The thing on its own had struck a chord. It made sense,
in spite of the fact that now, perhaps irretrievably, it opened
up to us a whole new aspect of raw, real life, which perhaps
could take a turn for the dangerous. It explained a lot of
small details about our neighbor that we hadn't taken the
time to pay attention to. Once it started getting around, you
could no more prevent yourself from being influenced by it
than if someone nearby you started yawning.

My brother urged me to look at things realistically. "Look
at this realistically," my brother said. "I never heard about this
lady, and if the FBI put someone into your neighborhood, I
would know about it because, they would have a computer in
their house, and I'd be the one who takes care of it. I would
also be the one who installed it."

"Maybe you wouldn't have told me."

"I would. I would tell you to move."

"If she isn't Witness Protection, she maybe was *almost*
convicted of something. Maybe she copped a bargain. Was she
convicted of something?"

"Sissy," my brother said. "You're my sister and I love you,
but do me a favor. Nip this thing in the bud. I swear on the
eyes of my kids, it's not true. You watch too many movies. If
she's in there, and the guys I know had something to do with
it, I would definitely know about it. I would definitely know.
You are talking to someone who would know about it."

"I bet you she's Italian," I said.

"You need to get a life, Sis."

"I've got one."

"You need to get a better one."

As soon as I hung up the phone with him, I tried to think
of someone I knew who I hadn't already talked to about this,

but I had talked about it to everyone. No one was left; I had saved my brother for last.

I made up my mind to go over to Garfield Street and see for myself what was there.

Her house was the second gray ranch on the left, that is, left as you're facing the woodlot that makes the street a dead end. Three or four months, I felt, was not too long a time to be living in a neighborhood before someone came over with a gift and said, "Now that you've had a chance to settle in, I came over to welcome you."

The gift I brought was a neutral one, it was an icebreaker. There is a bakery I like a lot, about a twenty-mile drive along the river from here, at the edge of an old mill town lower down in the valley. I'd been down there that morning and had bought the same thing I always buy there, a sour cream coffee cake. The bakery had run out of their usual boxes; so they gave me a plain brown one, which was more like a small carton than a cake box. But I hadn't had another box at home to replace it. As I carried it over to Mrs. Kamsky's, I could feel the cake sliding around.

I knew from our librarian that the addition to Mrs. Kamsky's house was nearly finished. What purpose it would serve, I didn't know, it was another mysterious thing. I wished I had thought to ask about it. I wondered if the Peetes were actually building Mrs. Kamsky a backyard deck, and by referring to it as an addition, what they meant was, it was very expensive, or it was showy and overly large, as you see sometimes, when enormous wooden decks fill a yard, like the playpens for children of giants, who must always stay away from the actual ground of the earth, and must never be soiled by grass stains.

Sometimes the people in our neighborhood who have these kinds of decks end up adding a roof or an awning. It can easily get out of hand. I wondered if the Peetes were making fun of Mrs. Kamsky when they called what they were doing here an addition, but when I turned the corner onto the Garfield Street sidewalk, I saw that I'd worried about this for nothing. From the front of the house, as well as from the frontmost part of both sides, you could see no addition at all. I took this as a positive sign. I went up the front steps to her door and rang the doorbell, which, and this didn't surprise me, didn't work.

"Excuse me, are you looking for me?" said the voice of a woman.

It was Irene Kamsky herself, standing on the bottom step, looking up. I had not heard her come up behind me. In her hands was a large metal watering can, slightly rusted; some water sloshed out when she set it down on the sidewalk.

It was July. She was barefoot; although the steps, and the cement of the sidewalk in front, must have been painfully hot, she didn't seem to notice. She wore a pair of baggy old tan Bermuda shorts and a long-sleeved white blouse with the shirttails out. Around her head she wore a pink and white speckled bandana, tied at the back of her neck. Her eyes looked like the eyes of someone who is weary, and who never quite gets the right sleep. She was fleshy and plump, like a fig. Her skin was very white. There were thick beads of sweat on her forehead and neck, but, like the heat, she did not seem to mind.

In case my brother had been lying to me, the first thing I said to her was, "I'm Elmo Gavoni's sister Sissy."

"Elmo," said Mrs. Kamsky. "When I was a girl, I knew a man called Elmo the Clown."

"Oh, it's not the same one," I said.

She came up the rest of the steps. She moved slowly. In features, and by the look of her skin, she looked as if she couldn't be older than forty-five or forty-six. But in the way that she carried herself, she looked older than I was. (I was just about to turn sixty.) Her left hand went automatically to her hip, with her elbow crooked outward. Favoring her other hip, she tipped slightly to the right, like a grown woman's version of a child, who's singing, "I'm a little teapot, short and stout."

That was the way she came up the stairs. There was nothing childish about her. There were only four steps, but it took her a long time. There wasn't a railing. Had Mrs. Kamsky been made from tin, I would have been able to hear her creaking. Had I been able to handle her weight, I would have put down my cake and picked her up. I'd've done anything for her. I felt this way from the first moment I saw her.

Then this was what she did. When she reached me, she pointed to the box in my hands. She slightly inclined the upper part of her body toward the box, but clearly, she was keeping her distance. She still was standing there like a teapot.

A long moment went by in which she looked at the box intently, turning her head this way and that, and when I couldn't stand it anymore, she smiled at me, as if to comfort or assure me, and some flickers of light came into her eyes. Her hand came up off her left hip. She bent her head a little closer to the box. She was listening to it. I don't know how she did this exactly. I have often tried to repeat it, when I am telling this story to my friends.

But I never get it right. She did something with her hands in the air. She did something with the look on her face. She did something with the angle of her shoulders, with the tip of her head, with her ears. I knew exactly what she was saying. She wondered if I had brought her a bomb. If I had blinked my eyes or looked away from her, I would not have been surprised, looking back at her, to find that she was dressed in a bomb squad suit.

"It's not going to explode on you when you open it. It's a sour cream coffee cake," I said.

"I'm so very pleased," she said.

Oh, I'll never get it right. She mocked me, but I didn't feel mocked. She tricked me, but the trick was a good one. That was how I met Irene Kamsky. The only resentment I ever felt toward her was this: when she listened to my box to see if it was ticking, I started thinking the same thing myself, and I couldn't understand how she had done this.

THERE WERE NOT many people on our street who could say a decent word, when the occasion arose, about that woman Mrs. Kamsky had working for her, Margaret Dunlap: dry-looking, sour-looking Margaret Dunlap, whose face was so sallow, and whose clothes were always so dowdy, and whose eyes were so void of expression, like the eyes of refugees in a war documentary on public TV, which you quickly have to change the channel on. But I liked her, even though the face she turned to us was a face of indifference. She barely ever stepped foot from Mrs. Kamsky's house and yard except to get off or catch her bus.

But even I myself could be heard now and then to admit to the possibility that, if I didn't know for a fact that Margaret Dunlap had come to Mrs. Kamsky from a certified agency, I would have to shake my head just like everyone else, and wonder, what is the world coming to, if this is the type of person getting jobs in the health care field?

Things had not been going well for Mrs. Kamsky since her hip replacement surgery. We left her alone. Of course we knew about the studio behind her house; we knew she gave dancing lessons, although rarely to the children of our friends. It was not an unusual thing, any more than my neighbor Julie Johnson owning four perfect golden retrievers, all male, and earning herself a small income on the side from studding. And the Hazeltons had a venture-capital business going on in their garage, and Nancy Mastromatteo had a catering business in her kitchen. Mrs. Kamsky had the right to do as she pleased. She had been living here long enough to have fixed for herself a place in our minds as a modern-day plumper version of Greta Garbo, who had seemed so tragic, and who was possibly insane, but who had made up her mind to live her life as a symbol of something, and not in an actual life. She wasn't like the rest of us, rubbing shoulders with the very same people all the time, who would say to you, "We're your neighbors," but in fact you could look at them and have the awful sensation that they were strangers; you would feel that you were living the life of someone who was not yourself, as though you'd stumbled into someone else's life a long time ago, and you could not imagine a way to get out. Getting out of it would be no simpler, or less impossible, than if the fragile silk blossoms and fruit on my sideboard had suddenly come alert, and were charged with life and photosynthesis, instead of threads from a silkworm.

IT WAS AN IMPULSE of mine to invite the fifth grade of my niece, Linda, the daughter of my brother, to my house, for afternoon tea.

The fifth grade was such a big one this year, my niece had decided to limit it to only the girls. The boys would have an outing of their own, to the Basketball Hall of Fame.

It was arranged that Linda would arrive with her fifth-grade girls on a Friday afternoon in October at twelve noon. The tea party was changed to a luncheon so that it could happen during school-time. The girls who wanted to join the boys' trip, which was held on a different day, were free to do so, and most of them, of course, chose both.

Every mother I contacted for advice about this luncheon had said the same thing: "How many grown-ups will be there?" Two of us had not been an acceptable number, but I lied and said, "Oh, some neighbors will be here."

I planned the meal and prepared it myself: a chilled squash soup to be served in my mother's Victorian tureen; sandwiches of pink salmon on bread sliced as thin as shavings of ice; macaroni and cheese done up to resemble a soufflé; two kinds of green salad. Chocolate mousse was for dessert.

It had seemed to me in the planning stages that a civilizing feeling of grace and good manners would descend on the girls at my table like the Holy Ghost, amid my napkin rings and good Italian glass bowls. There would be far fewer food fights after this in the school cafeteria, which Linda had been complaining about—in which case, as I maintained all along, it should not have been the girls who were invited here, but the boys. In fact, since the death of my husband, except for Elmo, I could not remember any time at all when a male crossed the threshold of my house.

Until the day of the luncheon, that is, when Margaret Dunlap came ringing my doorbell.

Mrs. Kamsky's red sportscar had suddenly appeared in my driveway—a little red antique foreign convertible. I believe it was a Fiat.

In the passenger seat, as though riding a car in a homecoming parade, there was a woman of thirty or so, with the most beautiful face I'd ever seen. Her head was tipped back. Her eyes were closed like the eyes of someone sleeping. And another car came inching up behind it, an ordinary little hatchback, and all its doors were flung open at once. Five big healthy teenage boys from Mrs. Kamsky's went running to the little red car.

The fifth-grade girls were thrilled and amazed, as if I'd arranged an entertainment. One girl said, "Are they going to pick up that little car?" And you had the idea that they could have.

The girl in the passenger's seat wore a gauzy white scarf around her hair, and the sunlight was on it, too. And there were leaves in the maple trees along the driveway that were especially yellow that year. There was a strange abundance of gold and yellow leaves. Even with the scarf on you could tell that the girl in the car had the kind of blond hair that Grace Kelly had. When she sat in front of a mirror and brushed it, she must have felt that she was brushing blond mink.

"I couldn't think where else to bring her," said Margaret, in my doorway. "And I don't think that anyone would allow her at the moment to be registered in a hotel, in her condition, you see. It's really a very great kindness of you. Don't call anyone, please, as I'm a health care aide."

"But Margaret, what exactly would her condition be?"

"It would be, that she very much needs to lie down somewhere and have a cold damp cloth put on her head."

"Is Mrs. Kamsky not home? How can Mrs. Kamsky not be home? Is she home and are you locked out? Should I pick up the phone right now and call her?"

In a calm enough way, Margaret soothed me. "Mrs. Kamsky is very much at home, which is the problem."

"Oh, then bring her in! Bring her in!"

Meanwhile, with the soup in the bowls barely touched, and with the laid-out table of china and silver looking suddenly unimportant, and with the chairs pushed back at odd, silly angles, the girls from my niece's fifth grade were being ushered through my big kitchen and out the back. Linda had no trouble herding them up: the back door opened onto the driveway, which every girl had figured out for herself. Linda said, "You went to all this trouble, and I believe that the girl in the car, whoever she is, is dead passed-out drunk."

I said, "What an awful thing for these girls to be looking at," but my niece told me not to worry about that. They would barely, she said, notice the girl at all; she felt sure of it.

There was a cool fall breeze coming in through my dining room windows. Some thrown-down napkins on the table ruffled lightly. The girls edged their way down the driveway holding back their shoulders and nudging each other and saying, "I never saw such a hunk as the redhead." Or they were saying, "Look at those quads," and, "Never mind the quads, check the buns," and, "I wish I had my camera." They were only ten years old.

There were some difficulties involved in moving the girl from the car. The seat was small and low-down. And the five boys among them had some things to work out about who would do what and stand where. The girl's eyes fluttered open in an unseeing way a few times.

The five boys carried her unhastily, carefully. The girl wore a silk pant-suit—it was loose, and a light shade of tan. As they took her from the car, the top of the suit slid up, and exposed the lower part of her bra. "Hang on," said a boy. He fixed the top back into place as if pulling down a window shade.

Carrying her up the steps, they barely tilted her. One boy, the shortest one, positioned himself at the back of her head as they approached the doorway. The doorway was a wide one, and there wasn't any danger of her head being bumped, or even grazed, but he held his hands to the sides of her head, lightly, barely touching her, as you'd hold the sides of a basketball, if you were just getting ready to twirl it on the tips of your fingers. In a quiet voice, he said, "This is the most I ever saw anyone so much out of it, really totally out of it, in all my life."

Then the girl was in my house. I ran to the closet and took out a sheet for my sofa. "What's her name?" I said.

"She's Lisette," answered a boy. "She's a ballerina."

"I *knew* it," I said. "Does she belong to Mrs. Kamsky?"

"She used to. She moved away to somewhere. To Oregon," another boy said. "But she just got back for a couple of days."

"She lives in Colorado, bonehead," said another boy.

"You might as well stay for lunch," I told them. "Seeing as how I have it."

She lay on my sofa. Margaret fussed over her. I began to arrange the chairs back into their places at the dining room table, as if no one had come in yet to sit down. I put napkins back into the napkin rings. Coming back to her senses, would the ballerina on my sofa peer into the dining room and imagine that the table was set for her? "She's fine, she's fine, look, she's sitting up," said Margaret.

"I have some very nice salmon," I said.

A girl called out from the yard, "Thank you for the luncheon, Mrs. Gavoni, but we have to go now!"

I could not decide if I should empty the soup from the soup bowls back into my silver tureen, then serve it again, as if new. The squash it was made from was butternut. It had a smell of deepness and nutmeg. When I picked up a bowl, I spilled a little soup on the tablecloth. I decided to leave everything where it was. A couple of nights ago, I had gone to the movies with my brother. In one of the scenes in the movie, some fishermen come upon a dead young woman, lit up for the scene like a goddess. Her murdered body was naked like a woman in a centerfold. She lay dead in the shallows of a clear, rocky stream, which glistened with water and light. A silvery sheen was all around her, as if it were raining with invisible, silver rain. A fisherman looking down from an overhanging rock caught sight of her. He stared at her a long moment, and then he unzipped his fly. He took aim, and he peed on her. Then he turned away to go fishing. He was out on a fishing trip with a few of his friends. He'd come up to the rock to pee.

I could not get this out of my mind. When I mentioned it to my brother, he said, "I can't believe they show that kind of thing in the movies now." He meant that they had shown an actor peeing.

This was what I thought of when Lisette came into my house. It had happened to me that, when I saw the way that boy had touched his hands to the sides of the ballerina's head, I felt as if my heart had stopped beating, exactly as though a clock had stopped ticking. When it started again, it had hurt. It was a sudden, sharp, lurching, terrible cramp. I could not remember the last time in my life when I had ever felt it move in quite this way.

I did the right thing by going into my bathroom until I was finished with crying all those tears. I did not want the ballerina to wake up on my sofa and then come out to the table and see a stranger there, a foolish-looking, teary-eyed stranger, standing around fussing with the plates, and looking as if her heart had been stolen.

marybeth

AT THE D.S. PRATT LABEL AND CONTAINER COMPANY there are three of us named Mary: Mary Jane Molinas, Marianne Viglioni, and myself, Marybeth Burgoyne, the Mary with the husband that was adulterous. We all work in the office. Mary Jane is administrative assistant to the floor manager, Marianne is chief of support to three sales teams and I'm with the supervisor of manufacturing. Everyone calls us "The Triplets." All three of us are close in age and in the next few years, we're turning forty and so is my husband.

Just because the adultery happened ten years ago is no reason to expect me to feel different about it. Inside, where a heart is, tells time in different ways, from how time goes by on clocks and calendars. If a ballerina could have a heart like people have, you would know this.

"Ballerina." It's a beautiful word. It makes everyone think of light and shimmery things like clouds and the moon, and things that are shiny and glittery, like dancing in the snow in *The Nutcracker,* which I had always loved to watch on television, every Christmas. A ballerina! I'd think of girls as fragile as porcelain, that are as skinny as a pencil, and their breasts never fully develop, and who never get periods, and are not all the way completely human. I thought of things that were gauzy, and alien and beautiful and tragic, and girls with their hair up in buns, girls wearing tutus, all anorexic, that people ought to feel sorry for. I thought of girls that live unreal exotic lives, like aristocrats and royalty and movie stars. I thought about a jewelry box I had when I was little (it was also a music box) that had a two-inch glass girl on the top, in a silver glass costume, and her feet were like a white crystal v. When the lid was opened, the glass ballerina was tipped over backward, but she never fell off. The tune that it played was "Somewhere My Love," from *Doctor Zhivago*. My boss and the other two Triplets all had told me that sometimes when I'm sitting at my desk, a funny look comes over me, and I start humming, or even singing this song. They'll say, "Marybeth, don't you know any other tunes?" I never heard myself humming or singing "Somewhere My Love" from my old jewelry box. But it used to go around in my head, and I'd hear it like something far, far away, always the same little tune: dah, dah, dah dum, dah dah dah dum, like a broken-off, tinkly bit of a waltz.

If I ever heard that tune again for now and all the rest of my life it would make me want to clutch at my stomach like someone who was about to be sick.

Nobody would ever dare say the word "ballerina" if I am in a room, that is, no one who is my friend. It never mattered that you've been gone a long time.

Us Triplets stick together. We live in the same neighborhood. Sometimes I would see the way the other Marys looked at my husband (when they didn't know I was watching). He would be up on our roof cleaning gutters, he'd be waxing his car in the driveway, he'd be in his shop with the door wide open, working on his metals. Their eyes would get soft, their voices would go lower, to whispers.

They couldn't help it. They would see him in the light of someone tragic and interesting, like a saint in a painting at church with a halo around his head. They would never have looked at him this way if you worked at the counter at Dunkin Donuts, say.

I tried so hard to fool myself that you didn't really drive by me. I kept up such a good composure. I was fine, I was doing my job, I was perfectly calm. We were jobbing for a company that makes yogurt. We were producing their containers. The container was supposed to be large enough to hold eight ounces. That's what it said on the label. Eight ounces.

Thirty-four thousand containers and thirty-four thousand lids, that were piled on skids and ready for shipment, had been made in a seven and three-quarters size. The difference in the size was something the operator of the machine had noticed, but not until the end of the job. He had happened to look at the label, after all the containers were made. The person who typed the numbers for the calibration of the machine was me. I don't remember putting down seven and three-quarters instead of eight. If all those containers went out to the yogurt plant as they were, this is what would have happened: the yogurt would be fed into the containers by machine, and the amount of yogurt going into each container would be, eight ounces. There would be leftover spurts of yogurt going everywhere, which they would notice, and we would never be jobbing again for that plant.

"Harry, destroy everything on those skids for the yogurt people, and don't ask me any questions," was what my boss the manufacturing supervisor had to say to the machinist. If I was a different kind of person I could have changed the calibration order. It wouldn't have been hard to make it look like it was the machinist's own fault. He was an alcoholic anyway, Harry Matherson. But I'm not the kind of person who doesn't own up to their own mistakes.

They won't fire me for this one thing. They will wait for a second miscalculation. But they'll look at me with different eyes. Did Marybeth Burgoyne make another mistake yet? Should we put Marybeth on probation? Can we trust this Marybeth?

In the break room on our late-afternoon break I put down my head on a table and cried for a while, not noisily, just wetly, just quietly, so the tears poured down my face and into my hands like rain. The other two Triplets thought that I was crying because my boss was going crazy over those thirty-four thousand yogurt containers, and they patted my shoulders, they smoothed my hair, they gave me kleenex, they said, "People screw up all the time, Marybeth. One mistake is not the end of the world." They said, "You are an honest, good person, Marybeth, unlike ninety percent of the people who live in this world."

It was just on the tip of my tongue to tell them that I saw you, or just simply, "Billy's ballerina came back." Why didn't I? They're my friends, my best friends, we tell each other everything, we're the Triplets, but seeing you again, Lisette, was something I had decided to keep to myself. I could pretend to myself I didn't see you. I could pass off the way I felt as being upset about a miscalibration of a setting of a machine, and upset about the way my boss was screaming about it. When it came to the other Marys, they would no more expect to hear about you again than they'd expect to see a ghost. You were a ghost to us. You were a bad dream. One of the other Marys asked me once if, if God walked into a room where I was, and offered me a choice between, would I rather have my husband be stricken with a terrible disease, or would I rather have my husband be unfaithful to me, which one would I pick? I would pick the disease. I don't care what you think of me for saying this. I would rush to find medical information, I would find him great doctors, I would become an expert on his disease, I would find a way to have him healed.

I would never have thought that I would ever see you again. And then suddenly you passed by me.

I was coming down the steps of the post office, having rushed there on an errand for my boss. You went by me in a red foreign sportscar.

I went as still as a statue when I saw you. A homely little Irish-looking woman was driving. The car was headed up Water Street. It turned at the lights and went out onto the road that led north into the suburbs. Later on I remembered that you used to have a teacher out there, who was vain about cars.

You were sitting in the passenger seat. You wore a white kerchief on your hair. Your head was tipped back. You wore a gold necklace. Did my husband make you that necklace? You seemed to be looking up at the roof of the car as though you saw right through it, as though something overhead in the trees had caught your eye. The leaves were so brightly yellow and gold this year. Maybe you had said to the driver, "I'd forgotten how much I loved this whole valley in the autumn."

Sometimes it happened to me after you had committed adultery with my husband, I would suddenly get the feeling that everything was somehow planned out for me ahead of time, as though I had to act a part, I had to say things and do things that I normally wouldn't. We were just like three sticks, put together as a triangle, when us other two sticks had been okay with each other just as lines.

And then everything felt so differently arranged. Did you ever get all dressed up and go and visit him in the machine shop, and then go back and tell your teacher funny anecdotes about it?

There's a commercial on TV where a tall ballerina in a white tutu starts twirling across a kitchen floor, and a pot of spaghetti sauce on the stove, which she doesn't know is there, boils over and spills: just as the ballerina is landing on the red puddle, a hand, holding a paper towel, shoots out from somewhere, and mops up the sauce in one stroke. The ballerina just keeps on doing what she's doing. It's a commercial for the paper towel. Do you know what my husband's face looks like when this picture appears on our screen? One time he said to me, "She's up on her points when she spins like that. That's what they call it. Points." But it was only that one time. He never said anything like that again.

And once when we were looking at stereo equipment in a department store there was a stereo on, a display, playing music from a symphony. I had noticed what it was like, but I thought I noticed it because the stereo on display was very expensive. Hearing the violins was like someone was playing violins on the inside of your ears. There was a salesman coming toward us and he took one look at us and went over to the stereo to change the music. He stopped the violins and put on *More Great Classic Hits of the Seventies* and the Eagles started singing "Hotel California."

But just before he did, I looked at my husband. I saw what his face was like. A flash was in his eyes, a spark, a quick spark, the way someone looks happy when they recognize something they love. It was like seeing someone with a light, an actual light, and a sudden quick heat and a jumpy bright spark. Naturally I would want to feel it too, as though Billy could pass over some of it to me, the way you'd hand someone a flaming stick from a fire you had, so they could start a fire of their own. "Firebird," my husband said. Those violins. "Firebird." He had whispered it. He was talking to himself. Is that what he had called you? I wonder if he had thought that you were magic. I wonder if you had put him under a spell. "Firebird." I pretended I didn't hear him. He wandered over to some other components in the shop. I said to the salesman, what was the name of the disc that was playing before, those violins? He didn't know, it was just a sampler from a record company. But the next day I called up a radio station that plays that kind of thing and I acted like I was doing research. They had put me through to someone in Music Reference. I said, "Can you tell me about a symphony with violins called 'Firebird'?"

"It's a ballet about a strange and wonderful bird," he said, and I hung up the phone while he was talking.

Billy still works at the same machine shop. Is that where you were going? Is that where you had come from? I will never know. He's got a shop of his own for nights and weekends in our garage now, too. He said that you never knew where we live. He said you were never at our house. Sometimes I believe him and sometimes I don't. It's about half and half, it's what you would call a balance. Did you dance for him or did you only just fuck him? He said, it was only a couple of times. He said, "If you never forgive me, Marybeth, even for all the rest of our life, I would still always want us to stay married."

He's not that good-looking of a man. He's strong, he's got dark big brown eyes, he's got a way of being quiet that, people like to go over and stand near him. "Still waters run deep" is what my mother said once when I had first brought him home. I had thought it would be the sort of "deep" where, I could be in it too, with him. Everyone likes my husband. Metalworkers have patience and strong hands, and they know what it means to have things in their hands that are molten and fiery and glowing and mysterious. Was that it? Did you like to be in his hands, were you shiny for him?

One time my husband and I were babysitting for Marianne Viglioni's little boy. She'd brought him over. We were watching *The Wizard of Oz*. It felt good to have a child in our house.

Maybe we'll have kids, me and Billy. I don't know. I don't know if it would be fair to a baby to have a mother who would only believe its father about half of the time. It would be something a baby would notice. "Mama does not trust Dad," would be its first conscious thought in the world and it would grow up to be suspicious and scared, like something I fed it, or something it acquired, in its genes.

We were watching *The Wizard of Oz* and I was making fudge brownies in the kitchen. The movie was at the part where they come upon the Tin Man. He gets oiled, he starts moving. The little Viglioni was four years old but he already had been hanging around my husband a lot in his shop, he was a budding baby metalworker, he would sit in the doorway and watch my husband at work like something in a movie. "Tin," he screamed. He started jumping around in our den. "Tin tin tin tin tin! Billy is the Tin Man! Billy is the Tin Man!"

My hands were mixing sugar and eggs in a bowl. I had looked in the doorway to see what the excitement was. My husband's face was suddenly flushed like someone with a sunburn. In *The Wizard of Oz* the Tin Man is the one who has no heart. It did not seem likely that Jeffy Viglioni would think of my husband as someone who had no heart. He was too little. He hadn't known my husband long enough to be able to understand this kind of thing. On the screen, the Tin Man was walking around. He was as intimate with metals as you can be. Is that what you had called my husband? Tin Man? Did you do it on purpose when you reached in his chest and took his heart, or had it happened accidentally?

We went to a marriage counselor. We did all the things that people do. I would never ask you, point-blank, to stay away from us. I wouldn't ask you, ever, for anything at all. I would never insult myself that way, no more, I think, than you would, if, looking at me in the eye, you asked me a trite, insulting question, like, "Oh, poor Marybeth, do you hate me?"

To tell you the truth, when I first caught sight of you, I disbelieved my eyes. I told myself it couldn't possibly be you. I told myself that it was probably one of those blown-up rubber females from a pornographic sex shop, which, as you may or may not know, get taken to the stadium for a football game like a rubberized date, with clothes put on it, so the guys don't get stopped by police—I mean the kind that, under the clothes, has rubber nipples, like on baby bottles from Playtex, and a hole between the legs, so I've heard, where a you-know-what goes, and there's lots of synthetic hair. Does it bother me to have pictured you this way? It bothers me not in the slightest. It was the first thing I thought of. I had hoped you were only a doll.

billy

WHEN EVERYTHING STARTED falling apart, and Marybeth was maybe divorcing me, and things with me and Marybeth were as low they could get, which was really, really low, she told me that Lisette had wanted to sleep with me because ballerinas hate normal married women, and to cope with their hatred, they kept trying to steal their husbands. They were just like spiders. She had felt that, sleeping with Lisette, I had been trying to send her a message.

Maybe I was depressed. Maybe I needed more attention but I could never come right out and say it. She would talk like this: "Being a guy, you can't talk right." Maybe we didn't have enough sex anymore, me and Marybeth, maybe I was just saying, "Have more sex with me." Or maybe I wanted to hurt her, for some reason, because she likes to take care of me and the house. Or maybe I wanted her to take *better* care of us, of me and the house, like me and the house were two equal people, was that it? Was she not taking care of us right, the house and me? I told her she was taking care of us just fine, but it began to seem to her that when I slept with Lisette, it had nothing to do with sleeping with Lisette. Sleeping with Lisette only had to do with the messages that Marybeth thought I was sending her. She always referred to it as, "slept with." It's probably not the right thing that me and Mary-beth are staying married. But that's what we're doing. I never should have told her about Lisette. I could have got through it okay if I hadn't told her. I could have told her instead (after it was over with me and Lisette), I was depressed all the time like a zombie for a different reason. I could have blamed it on my job, like maybe I hated my job. Or I was worried about money, or getting sick. I just had broken down with it one night. "There was this ballerina."

I DON'T KNOW if this happens to other people but when Marybeth and I first got married it wasn't anything like I thought it would be.

She would watch me, more than my own mother ever did, except for when I was small. The slightest little personal habit I had, she was on me about it, the slightest little thing you never even think about, never mind discuss with your wife, never mind be supervised. I'd come out of the bathroom. Maybe I'd been in there a little longer than what she thought was normal. She'd look at me and ask me, did everything come out all right?

I'd be going out the door to ride my bike. Did I have clean underwear on? Where was my helmet? What time was I coming home? Would I be very very very careful in the streets?

I'd take out a carton of orange juice. I'd pour some into a glass. Up she comes behind me in this way she has where, I never hear her coming. Maybe the glass is near the edge of the table. I pour the juice. Maybe I'm a little shaky from her coming up behind me and always spooking me. "Oh, I'll do that," she says. Takes the carton from my hands. Pours. Goes over to the sink. Picks a sponge up. Dampens the sponge at the tap. Wipes the carton on the sides where I was holding it. Folds the flap. Puts it back in the fridge. Watches me drink the juice.

"Honey," she tells me. "Make sure you rinse that glass before you put it in the dishwasher because that juice you always buy is so pulpy. I wish we could buy it from concentrate so it's thinner and never sticks to the glass." But I like it better with the pulp.

HER REAL NAME was Lisa Annette LeMoyne, so it wasn't the kind of thing, like everyone thinks, where the "Lisette" was fake or made up. She had decided to be a dancing teacher. There is not much call for dancing teachers in the world of today except aerobics, but there still are many dancing teachers.

AFTER IT WAS OVER with me and Lisette I fixed up the garage. Insulated it, put in double-pane windows, got a pretty good electric heater. On the side I started doing a little metal work. It's pretty easy to get equipment I need from the shop. It's nothing big-scale. It's mostly fixtures for houses, maybe a couple of boats now and then. Hinges, specialized pipes, fireplace and stove stuff, roof strappings—it's word of mouth, and I also have some deals with a couple of hardware stores where I can make them something faster than ordering it, and the customer doesn't mind the extra charge. What I end up making money on is the fact that there's something about saying "custom-made" that people get into, even if it's nothing but a couple of doorknobs. In the garage with all the workshop stuff are my mountain bike, my Trek racer, my three-speed old Raleigh, my other mountain bike, and spare tires and seats and lots of bicycle stuff, and a little fridge about the size of a cooler they threw out from the break room at work, and my stereo system that, if Marybeth knew how good a system it was, and if she ever found out how much I paid for it, or how the different components keep getting replaced, as I'm always looking out for good trades, she would look at me like I had caused it to happen to her that all the blood pumping out of her heart had just stopped, had just totally drained away from her. The income I get off the side goes into our bank account like my paycheck from the shop, but not all of it. My shop belongs to a credit union. They send over my statements to my foreman's office. Everybody who works on the floor at my shop has a locker in the basement, but when my wife comes to meet me after work, that's where we meet. My foreman's got a Harley that he keeps in the auto body shop of a friend of his, which his wife doesn't know about, so he's okay about letting me have a drawer for my statements and things in one of his file cabinets. In the garage, if I feel like climbing up on something and opening one of the windows and peeing on the dirt where nothing would ever grow, not even crabgrass (it does now), I go ahead and do it. I told her, "You can control the kitchen, the den, the bedroom, the bathrooms, the dining room, whatever, but this garage, Marybeth, is mine."

GETTING TOGETHER with Lisette was unpremeditated on every level. She wasn't even someone I'd look at twice if she and I were alone in an elevator or something.

Our last names rhymed. It was one of those coincidences. Burgoyne, LeMoyne. She was the first and only woman I ever made love to who was exactly my height. It took me a while to get used to what it felt like to kiss a woman in a standing position without bending my head down, and then, at the end of the kiss, to look at eyes that were level with mine. It was embarrassing at first, and I would always look away really fast. It felt like looking into a mirror, and the face looking back at you wasn't yours.

I WAS DOWN at the registry one day getting my license renewed. They take your picture and call your name. There weren't a lot of people waiting but things were slow. Actually, Lisette and I were the only people there. But I didn't look twice at her until the guy at the camera, a foreign guy, he could hardly speak English, I think this must have been his first day on the job, he called out from his booth something that sounded close enough to Burgoyne to make me think I could finally get out of there. He was standing there holding one license and shaking it in the air to dry off the lamination. And Lisette and I both got up at the same time to go get it from him. Our names rhymed. We bumped into each other.

She looked a little sloppy. She had faded old navy blue sweats on and a beat-up pair of Nikes. Her hair was in a really tight ponytail, not at all how it looks when it's down.

I had known right away from bumping into her that she was strong, she must have been some kind of athlete. I was surprised at how I almost lost my balance, which I hardly ever do. I said to her, something like, "You work out every day in a health club, or what?"

She said, "I work out all the time, I'm a ballerina."

I thought she was kidding. In the parking lot of the registry, we acted like, "Well, that was kind of dumb, but nice to meet you, and maybe I'll see you the next time you renew your driver's license."

I went over to my car. She went over to hers, on the opposite side. And the next thing I knew, we had both turned around, and we were both walking over toward each other again. I had made it back to my car about as far as the rear fender, and then my body went into a kind of u. All of a sudden, I was acting like a strange, slow-motion boomerang. I turned around and started back to where she was, and she was doing the same thing exactly.

It was obvious that the next thing I had to do was give her the number of the outside phone line in my foreman's office. So I did. I told her what times of the day would be best for her to call me.

I had wanted to go over to where she was. Going back to my car and getting into it and driving away, and not turning around, and not walking back over to where she was, these things were not a possibility for me.

There are three main divisions in how I've lived. First, there was a large block of time including everything that happened to me before Lisette, and then there was Lisette, and now there's the rest of my life. I'm okay about it. It happened that, there's my life, and in it, there was this one intermission. You go out to a show, you don't expect the intermission to be better than the show.

It was really only a couple of months between the time I met her and the time she left town. She had wanted to know if she should call me sometime, let me know what she was up to. I said, "No way."

a meeting

I WORKED IN the registrar's office of a small well-off college at the edge of a pine grove. It was a good job, and the campus had been endowed by a grateful alumnus with a lifetime landscaping contract. In the nonwinter months, something was always blooming, and in the winter, we had fields all around us of pines, pines, and more pines. The lawns of the college were as green and sleek as a golf course. Students who went here became medical technicians, law enforcement officials, marketing consultants, accountants, and business managers. It was difficult to flunk out at this college.

In an on-again, off-again way, I dated the registrar, who had been married for a very long time, but in an on-again, off-again way. It was complicated. I did not have children of my own. My older sister knew exactly what she was doing when she named her baby Robin. My own first name is Kathleen, and that's what the registrar calls me, and so does everyone else, but when I was a girl, my nickname was Robin. It came from Halloween one year when I dressed up as Robin Hood. I liked the costume so much, I was Robin Hood always, every year, until I outgrew Halloween. My costume had variations as I grew, and in the last one, I wore green tights, a green suede vest that I had found somewhere, a green turtleneck sweater, a child's toy bow which I wore on one shoulder like a book bag, and pointy-toed low suede boots that I had found in my mother's closet. I stuffed the tips with tissues until I could wear them for real. It wasn't that I loved to dress up as a boy. I loved to dress up as Robin Hood. I loved Robin Hood. I would watch the reruns of the old black-and-white TV show again and again, enraptured. I knew all the stories by heart.

My sister and her husband had not planned to have a baby. From the start of the pregnancy it had not gone well, and she was born about six or seven weeks prematurely. On the first night of her life I stayed in the hospital room with my sister and brother-in-law. I felt that I was lying at the bottom of a hole. She weighed two and a half pounds. I imagined other things of this weight: half of an oven-roasted chicken; the computer printouts of grades of full-time students at the college; a human heart.

I vowed that I would love her. My sister's house at that time was on a parallel street to mine. Looking out my kitchen window, I could see my sister's backyard and part of her roof. I thought we would live this way forever. I vowed that my niece, this new tiny Robin, would be as familiar in my house as my furniture. I pictured myself driving to the grocery store and bringing home all the things her parents would forbid her: real ice cream, potato chips, hot dogs, white bread and grape jelly, candy bars in boxes by the dozens. She would have to be accepting of the registrar. If he happened to show up on an evening we were watching TV together in the den, she would have to move over on the sofa to let him sit with us.

The baby lived and she was fed expensive formula. The downy dark hair she was born with fell off. Her eyes opened: she was like a creature who had come from the wild.

She was a fussy, difficult baby, and my sister and brother-in-law despaired because she never smiled. But when I entered a room where she was, a light would come into her eyes, and she would arch up her back and know me as a thing in the world that breathed and was warm and adored her. She was dark-haired and her features were blunt and homely. Her nose was small and flat, her eyes were what my sister called "mousy," her ears stuck out and seemed a bit too large for her head. From the start she was always in motion.

When it was time for her to start crawling about in the normal infant way she didn't crawl; she would only move vertically. A hallway would stretch before her and she would disdain it because she wanted to climb up the walls. The fault was my own. I was always lifting her. I was always putting her into the air. I would place her on a bookshelf and let her jump. She rode on my shoulders like Thumbelina on a pony. I put her in a backpack and brought her to work with me and she'd be put on the counter and allowed to roll off into a box of shredded paper.

The registrar was in a period of "I'm trying to make a go of it with my wife," and never complained, not when he tripped on diaper bags and bags of toys and the waste-baskets smelling of Pampers, and he was forced to play the part of second fiddle. He was gracious about it. The other two women in our office were grandmothers. They would pass her back and forth and let her climb on the copy machine. She slept on the windowsill beside the potted geraniums like our cat.

To say that she was not a pretty child is to say that a nestling with a wide open mouth is not a bird. When she was brought out walking in the gardens of our college, she zoomed for the trees, for the flagpole. Students stopped to pet her, the faculty petted her, everyone petted her; someone was always picking her up. She did not know the meaning of physical fear. She felt herself excluded from the laws of normal life, such as gravity. I thought she might be in the Olympics one day.

She was four when there was trouble in my sister's marriage. There were storms, fights, business problems, raw nerves, recriminations: but my sister and brother-in-law, instead of divorcing, moved away. In the wake of their battles with each other, they came to realize that the two Robins were pretty much sticking it out together.

They noticed the way she would leap on my body and cling to me, the way she lit up her eyes when she saw me, the way she shrieked with joy when I swung her about, all over the house, in the yard, in circles and circles and circles, my wild beloved little thing, my little monkey, my little bird, my small part-bird and part-monkey. "It is a terrible thing to wake up one day and find out that your child was stolen from you by your own sister," my sister said. "You came between me and my baby and you turned her against me." I did not understand the bitterness that came into her heart. We sounded like people on a television talk show. They moved to a suburb about a half-hour drive away, farther north up the valley, near the hills. I was no longer welcome in their house except for Christmas and Easter and our birthdays.

The registrar never came with me on these visits. My sister and brother-in-law did not approve of the registrar. I think they found it weak of me to have kept things between the registrar and myself as they were, for so long: and perhaps they thought it would set a bad example for my niece. I was not in a position to put up a fight. It frightened me that my sister and brother-in-law might lock my niece in her room when I came; I might never be able to see her.

Never see her! It would be worse for me than if I never saw sunlight. I would close my eyes and think about the way she looked, in other days, coming to see me, running toward me in her hopping, springy way, with her arms swinging out, with her head held up high, with her face elated by the feel of rushing air, with her feet barely touching the ground. Never see her!

I would say to her, "Just because you can't see me very often, doesn't mean I'm not here." She would whisper, as I bent down to kiss her, "Well, I talk to you all the time. Just because you can't hear me, doesn't mean I'm not talking to you, all the time."

UPON THE RETIREMENT of the woman in my office who held the job of assistant registrar, I was promoted in her place. The registrar and I began traveling together for two or three days at a time, to motels in Vermont or by lakes in New Hampshire. We traveled around the country several times a year to conferences of community college administrators, where in front of everyone, we shared one room and passed ourselves off as a couple. The registrar became good at giving talks, and so did I.

This time, a conference was being held at a large, resort-like hotel near the Rhode Island border, and we could have made it there easily in a car for day trips.

The hotel was spread out over four acres, and that was only for the main building and the parking lot. It had a golf course, two ballrooms, its own nightclub and restaurant and snack bar and bar, and there were two indoor pools, four weight rooms, and saunas in all the bathrooms. A few people at the college had felt that college money should not be spent so freely on me and the registrar staying overnight at a conference we could get in the car and drive to, but we had been looking forward to this hotel for a long time. We had watched it being built on our drives together on lunch hours, in the registrar's car. It had risen from the ground where an army base used to be, like a modern-day Shangri-La. We had watched it go up the way children watch a playground being made at the end of their street.

I must have thought I would be happy if I could go there like I was walking away from the world, and everything I could want would be there. The registrar and I did not have too much trouble convincing the officials at our college to pay our bill.

Our room was on the third floor at the back. There was a tiny balcony that looked out on an oval pond. In the pond were goldfish: indolent, bloated goldfish, left to grow abnormally large. They were terrible to look at, they were grotesque; they swam up and down the pond in a strange, lazy slow motion, as if the slightest quick move would make them burst.

In the moonlight, in sight of a clear, sharp half-moon straight up above the edge of the golf course, I stood on the balcony and wondered why I had wanted to come here. I looked down at the pond.

The water was silver, like a sheet of aluminum foil. "What are you doing over there?" said the registrar. He had just come out of the shower. A damp towel was around his neck. He looked like a happy man.

"I'm trying to see the goldfish," I said.

"Oh, for crying out loud. The one morbid thing in the place," said the registrar. And just then, as he spoke, it became obvious that someone was on the balcony beneath ours. A woman. Her voice floated up to us as if it came from the air itself. It was not a voice I'd ever heard before, but I knew, somehow, the way you know these things, that it was the voice of a stranger who would not remain a stranger to me for much longer.

It startled me, it rattled me, it delighted me. "Oh, you are looking at the fat old fish? So am I, my dear. So am I!"

That was how I came to meet Irene Kamsky. I met her before I saw her. And though I felt at the time a rush of embarrassment and annoyance at being caught like that, unguarded, as if she'd spied the registrar and me making love, it passed quickly.

THE LOBBY OF THE HOTEL was also a lounge. The registrar and I sat down at a tiny table. We ordered scotch and held the glasses in our hands. A thin man in a plaid sports shirt and tan pants played medleys of tunes. An expensive gold watch was on his wrist. He played songs by James Taylor, Billy Joel, the Beatles, and Carole King, and the registrar was not embarrassed to sing some of the songs out loud, along with many other registrars from other schools.

A woman came over to our table and I knew that it was the same woman whose voice I had heard on the second floor balcony.

No—not "came over." I looked over my shoulder because I thought I was sitting near an air-conditioning vent, which had just been turned up to a higher setting—not a colder one; it wasn't chill that I felt; just a slight, pushing change in the air, and I turned around and looked up.

She was small, she was short, she was plump—not too much, just a softness all around of added-on weight, like someone bundled in extra layers of clothes. I guessed her age to be sixty or sixty-five. Her skin had an unnatural pallor as if she'd been ill. She did not sit down at our table although I invited her to.

She reminded me of someone, or of something—of someone or something in a dreamy, vague way, like a memory I couldn't quite place.

She stood by my elbow in a still, quiet way, and there was something in the stillness that made me think of things that are rooted into the earth in ways humans are not: trees, potatoes, a bush, and flowers that come from bulbs. She held one hand on her hip with her fingers flat against it, the way women who are even a little bit pregnant are always putting one hand against their belly.

She wore a white chiffon scarf on her head and it was tied,

turban-style, at the back of her neck, like a movie star from the nineteen forties and fifties. She wore an awful rayon violet-colored blouse and loose rayon slacks, the same color. A white puffy cashmere sweater was on her shoulders like a short white cape. She wore no makeup, and no jewelry.

"Don't tell me you're a registrar," I said to her.

"I won't. I may tell you I've come here because I want to work on my golf game."

"So did I," said the registrar. He smiled at the woman the way he smiles at students he spots in hallways who amuse him, with spray-painted green hair or earrings put into their nostrils. They amuse him but he also feels sorry for them. He had been drumming his fingers on the table because he didn't know the words to "Fire and Rain." The only part he knew was the chorus.

His confidence came back because the next song was "Barbara Ann." The registrar in his younger days had been deeply Beach Boy-like in appearance. He came from a suburb in Connecticut, but even now, he could make you think of him as an aging, perhaps tragic, former surfer, whose inner eyes were always scanning an ocean for waves. He was fit, very fit; he was proud of his physique; he had a stomach as flat as a board; and he still wore his hair like a Beach Boy, although the sides were going gray.

"He's very handsome," Mrs. Kamsky whispered to me (although I didn't know her name yet).

"Thanks," I said. The registrar knew that she was talking about him, but not what she said, and he blushed.

The piano was being banged by the pianist. The registrar put a goofy look on his face, as if saying—because Mrs. Kamsky had made him self-conscious—"I really think all of this is stupid, but I have to act like it's fun." He joined in with the other registrars. They sang, "Bah-bah-bah, bah-bah-bah-ran," at the top of their lungs, and the woman said something that astonished me.

"I know your little monkey," she said. "Your little monkey comes all the time to my door."

I must have looked to Mrs. Kamsky like someone deaf and dumb. She laughed at me, not unkindly, not mockingly, not nervously, just tickled with herself to have made me speechless in a riot of noise. The registrars sang louder, they were trying to drown out the piano.

Mrs. Kamsky's voice in my ear—she had kept leaning in closer to me—was like listening to a whisper in a tornado. "I teach. Your little monkey comes looking but does not come in."

She continued holding one hand at her hip. The color of her blouse and pants made me think of Easter baskets.

I said to her, "Are you a gymnastics teacher?"

"Oh, no, oh, my goodness," said Mrs. Kamsky. "Oh, what a kind thing to say!"

"Are you a tutor for school?"

My niece's idea of doing well in school was to receive a passing grade on everything to keep her teachers off her back, and then read and think about whatever she wanted, and pretty much keep it to herself. She often received cs and ds for effort, but she didn't care. They only counted real subjects in an overall average, which determined if you could pass to the next highest class. Classes in school were what children had to endure, to get outdoors twice a day and swing on bars in the playground. This was something that worried my sister and brother in law.

"If I were a tutor for her schoolwork, I would not be here speaking to you. I would be walking down the sidewalk and speaking to Patricia and Owen."

Patricia and Owen were the names of my sister and brother-in-law. It came to the end of the song. The piano player said into his microphone, "Catch you again in five, folks," and stood up and walked away to take a break. There were ironed-on creases down the front of his pants, perfect lines, perfectly unwrinkled, as sharp as the edges of paper, and I couldn't figure out how this was possible, when he'd been sitting at the piano with his knees bent for at least an hour.

The registrar saw some people he knew near the bar. "I'm going over to the bar," he said. "If you're going to talk about me anymore, wait till I come back." He acted as if every hotel he and I had ever gone to, and every conference, Mrs. Kamsky had always turned up, just like this, in every lounge. He liked her. He didn't make faces behind her back as he walked away. Mrs. Kamsky touched my shoulder.

"Let's go and have a little walk by the pond, you and I," she said. When I got up from my chair, I felt a little wobbly from the scotch, and she held out her arm to me, as people do when someone stumbles. I had one quick moment of panic, with the feeling that I was being taken away against my will, as a strange, resort-hotel hostage; but there was no way on earth I wouldn't have followed her.

THE GOLDFISH in the moonlight hardly moved; they looked like things from a nightmare.

There was a bench near the pond. Piano music skittered out from the hotel across the lawns. Somewhere in the shadows of the golf course, sprinklers were on, and water was hissing and spraying.

I wondered if I was drawn to the goldfish because there might have been a connection between them and the registrar, in spite of how healthy he was. Or a connection between a wrong size of fish, and the way that I was living my life. Or a connection between the way I thought things should be, in general, and how things really were.

Goldfish should be tiny and quick and shiny and alert, in a fishbowl. These were only passing thoughts. I'm not sure I would have had them if I were alone.

The hotel was lit up like a giant cake. The revolving big front door was like an upright, gold-painted tin can, going round and round and round.

I sat on the bench with Mrs. Kamsky. Again it occurred to me that she stirred in me some sort of memory; again, I couldn't get it clearly, as one hears a bit of music—just a small, fleeting piece, from the radio of a passing car, say, and you know it's familiar, but you can't remember what it is.

It was a good wood bench, solid oak, with a strong high back, the kind of bench that goes up behind you to your shoulders, and you can really sit back and lean against it.

But Mrs. Kamsky sat instead at the very edge of the seat, and I wouldn't have thought that a person as plump as she was would want to do this.

Her back became straighter; she drew back her shoulders and held up her head, and it seemed that for very long moments, her eyes didn't blink, although of course they must have. Her hands were lying flat on her knees, palms down, and her knees were pressed closely together, and her feet were flat on the ground.

I could not believe that she was comfortable in this position at the edge, but all the same, I felt that if someone were to sneak up behind us and pull away the bench, I would fall on my face in the dirt, and Mrs. Kamsky would just keep on sitting there, in empty air.

She held out her arms a little, as if shrugging, although her shoulders didn't move. She moved one foot behind the other, quickly, and then again, but a little more slowly. If you want to spell a word in the air, this is what you do with your fingers. The registrar would catch my eye in the office and do this, and if someone else noticed him, he'd clown it up, he would pretend that he was conducting a band.

He'd say, "I wish I could wear my walkman at work, but it wouldn't set a good example." He would spell out whole sentences, such as, "Kathleen, Kathleen, you're the dream of my dreams, and, "Let's get in the car and run away," and, "U, R, the 1 thing 4 me."

Behind Mrs. Kamsky, across the lawn, doormen in handsome gray suits were lounging against the wall smoking cigarettes. They snapped to attention and tossed the butts on the sidewalk and stamped them out whenever someone was coming or going. Sooner or later the registrar would come outside, squinting into the shadows, looking for me.

The last time I saw my niece, it was Easter. My sister had dressed her in a dark pink, big-skirted velveteen coat and a matching little hat, and a flowery dress with a stiff white collar.

It was like looking at a monkey that someone had dressed with doll's clothes. But my niece behaved well—she was going to be taken by my brother-in-law to a circus.

All she had to do was get a grade of B on her next report card in one subject, any subject she wanted, and she would be taken to the circus. In math, there were important weekly quizzes. She scored one hundred percent on the first six quizzes of the term, then failed all the rest of them, and ended up with a round solid B. She was going to be looking at a trapeze.

I remembered the way she held up her arms in the air when she told me this. "My dad's taking me to watch what they do on a trapeze." Her head had tipped back, her little hat slipped back. My sister ticked off on her fingers all the things one sees in a circus besides trapeze acts. Clowns, lions, elephants, ladies and girls in shiny, glittering costumes; jugglers, tigers, dancing bears, acrobats, beautiful white horses with ribbons tied into their tails.

But the trapeze is at the top of the tent, and the roof is only one sheet of canvas. You can't go any higher than a trapeze, except up through the roof, into clouds and air and stars.

I said to Mrs. Kamsky, "How did you find me, and what do you want me to do?"

She took from a pocket of the violet slacks what appeared to be a standard white business card, but it was just an old index card torn in half. In thin, light handwriting, it said, "The I. Kamsky Studio of Ballet." An address was there, too, just a number and street.

I recognized the name of the street and as I did, I remembered what she reminded me of. The street was just around the corner from my sister and brother-in-law. I must have looked at Irene Kamsky's house at Christmas and Easter many times, without ever wondering what was there, or what it would mean.

She reminded me of Miss Peggy Lee.

Suddenly, as though all these intervening years had fallen away, I could hear it coming again from the little transistor radio, cobalt blue, that my mother and father had bought me for my eighth or ninth birthday. In a babble of cheap AM talk shows, of "elevator music" and "champagne" tunes from Lawrence Welk, and a burst now and then of the new rock and roll, of which, when it was said, "It was the first time American youths made use of their pelvis openly," they weren't kidding, there rose to my ears the voice of the greatest American singer there ever was, Miss Peggy Lee, singing her famous song about disappointment and sorrow. It's the one called "Is That All There Is?"

Is that all there is?
Is that all there is?

If that's all there is, my friends,
Then let's go dancing.

In the downstairs den on a Saturday evening my mother and father in a rare bit of family harmony waltzed with each other between the sofa and the television set while Lawrence Welk conducted his orchestra and bubbles were coming from the bubble machines, as though all violins, when bows touched them, produced bubbles along with sound. My sister would clap her hands and whirl about and cry out, "It's so pretty!"

But for me, in a corner of the room, they were insubstantial, for nothing was there in that room except myself and the voice of Peggy Lee. The voice of Peggy Lee was as pure as the sound of a thrush when it's singing to the sun as though dawn were the worst thing that could happen (because it would mean another tomorrow) and the best, both at once (because it would mean you'd gotten through another night, somehow). It rose amid the cackling, whining, lesser birds, always sure of itself, and a little hungover, perhaps, and a little bit boozy. It was smooth and luxurious.

I think she had been put on this earth to explain what a heart was and, having taught you the lesson, broke it. She had the purest voice that was ever put into a human throat. I knew what she looked like from *Life Magazine*. I had wanted to grow up to be exactly like her, but I had not known how I would ever go about it. I had no voice at all. When I sang I would sound like a frog.

Now on the bench in the moonlight Mrs. Kamsky brought all that back, and I'd be saying a fib if I said it didn't thrill me to have her lead me, straight as an arrow, to, of all things, Miss Peggy Lee. My heart felt as light in my chest as though that voice had never left me, but was only just waiting to be stirred.

doreen

SOMETIMES when you're going out with a boy, you get used to how they wrap up their personal self: it's the last thing they'd think of showing to their girlfriend. They think they look better if they're bland and voided out, like at the core of their soul, all they are is a Ken doll. You have to wonder if they have a soul like everyone else, and if there's a core to it.

Kids went over to someone's house or the mall, and me and Davey, when everyone started getting into pairs, we'd end up with each other. It was a process of natural selection. We'd always be the only two left except for the kids who were still holding out on not having sex yet, which was a category neither Davey or me would belong to.

Just like everybody else who knew Davey, I figured that he'd get through high school okay, he'd maybe be on the track team or wrestle or something, and then he'd go to County Voke for the carpentry course, and go to work for his family, who were builders, and that would be that for Davey Peete. Probably, around twenty or so, he would marry some girl who wouldn't mind it how quiet he was, and how into being private he was. They'd have a whole bunch of kids. But I would feel so sad and empty inside, when I looked into the future, and pictured myself as someone whose boyfriend wasn't Davey, I imagined that whenever I came back here to visit, in my grownup faraway life, Davey and I would get together, and it wouldn't be adultery, either, because, whatever went on sex-wise with Davey and his wife, and whatever went on with me, whatever we did, me and Davey would have done it together first, and I happen to think that this is something that matters. It probably matters more in the long run than any marriage. But Davey's been acting strange and all closed up inside, completely closed up, like I can't get anything out of him at all.

I tell him, Davey, you're my boyfriend, I did it to you, you have to tell me what's going on with you. He says, no, I did it to you, and I'm like, This is how it is. You want to know what I am going to be when I grow up? I am going to go to work in a lab in a biological research center, a rich and famous one, where there's no guys and we are going to develop the next level of evolution. If there's guys in the lab because you have to have guys if you want to get money from the government, we won't tell them what we're really doing.

We are going to make it happen that nobody has any testosterone except the minimum. After we get done with that, if a guy wants a hard-on, first, he has to be a halfway decent sort of person, he has to earn it.

The basic problem with the biology of a guy is that they should have been programmed real different a long time ago. They should have had retractable dicks, completely retractable, like they'd retract into some kind of internal pouch, like they had a little button down there, and anyway, they'd be a lot better off if their scrotum was inside, all protected by, like, an extra rib cage, a tiny little miniature set of ribs. You really have to wonder sometimes like I do what kind of a race the human race would have already evolved to by now if the guys had all their stuff tucked inside them, not that I'm saying girls are perfect. It is completely unbelievable to me that the first-ever women who ever lived, when they were back in the caves, how they let it get by them that the guys went around with these dicks. It's like there's all these prehistoric rabbits in a hole in the ground, and half the rabbits are saying, "All you other rabbits, go stand in the corner and be quiet, because we're building big sticks to come and clobber you with," and the rest of the rabbits are saying, "Oh, sure, whatever you want."

In other words, what I'm trying to say is, it's not just the fault of a guy. It's partly simple biology, and girls were there, too.

"Okay, Doreen, let's just say we fucked each other," Davey says, and things get all right again between us for a while, and I say, "Tell me what's the matter with you."

He gets this totally serious look on his face; I never saw him look like this before. "Come on, I want to show you something."

He's got his brother's work truck. He's not supposed to be driving. He won't be old enough for a license for two more years, but you grow up in the construction business, you start getting behind wheels when you're like eleven. You learn how to place yourself outside of certain laws. There was not a cop in the valley who would ever have stopped a vehicle a Peete was driving, because cops had houses, and every cop around here either had some work done by the Peetes, or they'd need a Peete sooner or later.

Davey and I drove out of town, right down Main Street, by the post office, by the park, by the police station. We went north up the valley. We hardly had anything to drink: one can of beer apiece, and a tiny joint the size of my baby finger, so we were totally unscrewed up.

It was about ten o'clock at night, a Friday night. It was November. This half moon was coming up above the trees as the truck climbed up the hills. It must of been one of the brightest, whitest half moons I ever saw. Sure, your eyes would know from science that the light wasn't real, it was all like basalt up there, it was all just reflected off the sun, but so what. If that moon had been a full one we wouldn't've needed headlights.

139

I sat in the cab of the truck all the way over on the seat across from Davey. We were quiet. We didn't have the radio on. This was the first time we were somewhere with a radio and it wasn't on.

"Where you taking me, Davey," I asked him.

"Go along with me on this, because there's something you gotta know." All of a sudden it felt like there's two different modes in how life is. There's all the fooling around kind of stuff where you're going around mostly waiting for your real life to happen. And then there's like, something serious.

I liked the way it looked from the truck that the trees were bare of leaves. You could see more moonlight this way.

We went into a suburb I'd never been to. When he pulled up in front of this little house, where all the lights were out, I had the thought that he was going to rob it.

"I rob houses," was maybe what he wanted to tell me.

A car was in the driveway and it wasn't just an ordinary car. It was a maroon two-seater Porsche, I think, a convertible, as antique as anything, in great shape. Even with how dark it was you could tell it was really expensive. Something that old should have had a lot of rust and it shouldn't be shiny. The house was not that much to look at, but that car, it was as good as hanging out a sign that said, "Whoever lives in this house, they do not have problems with money."

Davey's face in the light from the streetlight was excited and he was trying to hold it in, and he seemed a whole lot older to me, like he'd just put on five or six years. He looked more like his brother Jimmy, whose truck this was, than like himself. Everything was weird for a minute like in *The Twilight Zone*. You could almost hear that theme song playing, all tinny and creepy, but then it was all right.

"The lady who lives here is fast asleep. She goes to bed every night at like eight-thirty, and the ballerina that's visiting her, she's staying at a motel," Davey said.

One thing Davey knew about me was that I was never very good at going along with things that other people had thought up. I'd go along for maybe a little while, and then I'd think up something better, and I'd be saying, oh, let's do it my way now.

"Davey, what ballerina? What are you talking about?"

"This ballerina," he said. "But never mind about her, she's like thirty or forty, she's old."

"Don't tell me what to not be minding about, Davey."

"Okay, but listen, because, I swear to God, Doreen, if you do everything right now the way I ask you to, then, I'll be the best boyfriend to you that you could ever imagine. Every other girl you ever knew, they would never have a better boyfriend than you would. Whatever you think up for me to do like a test or something of how good I could be at it, just give me the test and I'll pass it."

This was the most words put together at once that he ever had said to me. "You're already a pretty good boyfriend, Davey."

"Thanks," he said.

I said, "If someone's a ballerina, I feel sorry for them, and you better feel sorry for them too, because, they have really sicko eating disorders, they weigh like ninety pounds."

"Yeah, sure, but this one's not that big of a deal, she just visits this lady."

"What's her name?"

"Lisa or something."

"Davey, you know a ballerina? How can you know a ballerina?"

"Because of this lady," said Davey. "Close your eyes. No, don't just shut them. Put your hands on them, both hands."

I did. I heard Davey get out of the truck. After what felt like a long time, he came over to my door and opened it and leaned toward me. When I started to open my eyes he whispered, no don't, and he took hold of my hands and pulled them toward him, like to the zipper of his jeans. If he had wanted us to make love with each other right now, in the road, in front of some lady's house, I was willing to go along with it.

"Feel," said Davey.

He had taken his jeans off, and I'm like, "Davey, have you got *tights* on?"

"Yeah," he said. "You can look now."

He still had his old scruffed up brown leather jacket on, wide open and pushed back a little from his shoulders, and he still wore his same old T-shirt. But in place of the jeans were black tights. On his feet were white socks and black ballet shoes with a strap across the foot.

Tights, shoes, tights. Davey, another Davey, not the one I just rode in a truck with, but a Davey in tights and ballet shoes, stood on the sidewalk with his arms by his sides and with his feet spread out a little. I liked it how, inside the tights, his whole dick wasn't like this boring old rod or something, this like, ugly old turkey-neck biological piston or something. In the tights, it was like this mound. It was lumpy and smooth put together, and it was all rounded off. I liked the way it felt to shut my eyes again and put my hands there. Davey said, "I kind of go to dancing school for like, ballet." Then he said, "Doreen?"

"What."

"Nobody knows about this."

"I won't tell," I said.

"The lady that lives here, she's my teacher. The studio's around the back, and you know who built it? My dad and my uncle. Come on. There's a door at the back she never locks."

What he had in mind for me was to follow him around the house to the back. I think he had wanted to bring me into the studio and dance for me. His jeans and his shoes were on the curb. He picked them up and put them into the truck.

"Davey," I said. "Let's get out of here."

He looked at me from over his shoulder. His face and his eyes were partly at the point of looking hurt, and partly at the point of, maybe nothing will hurt.

"I want to get out of here," I said.

"Doreen, it's okay as long as we don't wake her up, she doesn't care who goes in the studio. She expects it."

"But I don't want to," I said.

And right about then we stopped looking at each other kind of closely, like into each other's eyes, which we had kind of been in the habit of doing, when we were out somewhere like this by ourselves. But he saw that I wasn't fooling around or getting nervous for nothing. He looked away from me.

I was saying to myself, "He knows a ballerina." I couldn't help it. I couldn't make myself picture a ballerina at all. There wasn't anything specific I thought of, except, "ballerina," and I was thinking, oh, I am not the only person who gets to be with him, in those tights. I went cold, or something.

All of a sudden we were shy with each other. I don't know how to explain how it happened that I wouldn't go along with him. It was like, I don't know, I wouldn't be able to stand it, or something. I didn't have a choice.

It was a physiological thing. One minute I think, oh, he looks so good in those tights and those shoes, and, oh, good, my boyfriend wears these tights, and the next minute I was saying, "Davey, put your pants back on and take me home."

Maybe sooner or later I might start to imagine what Davey looked like if I'd gone in there with him and watched him dance. Maybe it's the kind of thing where, if I was a little older, I'd be able to handle it better.

It was just like this barrier of coldness or something came up around me. I knew how much I hurt him. It was like I could measure it. But knowing that I was hurting him didn't stop me from doing the hurting.

It was like, I guess that just about wraps it up for me for having Davey Peete as my boyfriend, and I was right. I didn't even say to him, "Dance for me another time."

shaun

THE SON OF A BITCH broke my knee. It's not the worst thing that could happen. In the hospital I was the best-off patient they had. They had cancer people, people from car wrecks, a guy who got stabbed, three or four girls who got beat up real bad, and this was just on my end of the floor. You can get cut off real quick from what the outside world is like. You crossed over the line that divides the people who are out there walking around, from the ones that aren't.

Everything you knew about from before you crossed over the line, it doesn't do you any good.

When it comes to groaning sounds and suffering, and people crying and yelling, especially at night, all night long, you start imagining what's going on with them. Stuck in a bed, tied down by tubes, you'd probably imagine things a whole lot worse than they are.

This wasn't a hospital in a war zone or something, or some country with plagues, or some big weather disaster. It was a normal little American unimportant place, no big deal. The other patients wished that they were me because I only had something wrong that was like, it was only a few smashed bones, it was only this joint gone off its hinges. Like I said, I was the best-off patient they had. But the son of a bitch broke my knee. The son of a bitch *unhinged* me.

Before, my whole life was like a door in a door frame on hinges. They used to be pretty good ones. They were really in there solid. You'd push against this door, you'd expect it to open up for you to more life, not a nightmare.

Stuff for me in general now is all different. I don't know, maybe it'll come back sometime to how it was.

It doesn't feel it. It used to be, I didn't know what it was like to be on the other side of life. But then I went into this other side. I'd look at my mom and my dad and my brother, and they'd be telling me, "Shaun, Shaun, hang in there, hang in there." It felt like they were somebody else's family.

Maybe in the hospital they gave me too many drugs. I should've kept quieter about what the pain was like. But anybody who ever went through this kind of thing, probably most of them worse off than I was, would know what I mean when I say, when my knee got kicked out, I couldn't understand how everything else got shattered too.

I'd be zoned out on all these pills. You can look at someone, and they can be completely high, completely wasted, and you don't know it, unless they're so far out of it that their tongue is hanging out. Their eyes are way too shiny. I'd look at myself in the metal lid they put on your tray, like it was a mirror. I'd think, maybe my eyes look so shiny because this lid's so dulled-out and old.

When I could get up and go in the bathroom where a real mirror was, I had to make sure I didn't turn the light on. If I was a raccoon or a skunk or a black or brown dog on the side of the road one night, and you drove by me, and you didn't see my shape, but your headlights lit up my eyes, you'd get a little spooked out, you'd be going, that really freaked me, and that was what my eyes were like in the bathroom mirror and in the lid they sent up with my food.

The first thing that went was all the edges of stuff. I never knew that so much stuff had all these edges. All of a sudden, there was a camera inside my brain, and the focus screwed up. All the edges of all the stuff I'd be looking at, they'd blur out.

Blurred: you could get the hang of this real quick.

You could see the attraction. Something's got edges, hey —get rid of the edges.

Sometimes it was like, on all the drugs I was on, my body was in a bathtub or a pool, but not in water. It was body-temperature mercury or something. I'd be sitting back relaxing in this great liquid silver stuff. Or I'd be looking out the window at some clouds, when the clouds were really low ones, and I'd be going, how come they go right by my window and don't come in here.

After the edges of things start going away you find out that it's like, someone drew a picture of the world with a pencil, and that's the world.

The worst thing about it, when everything gets all gray and gray-white, and nothing else is around but maybe some shadows, is how you start to get thinking, "This is like, the real thing."

You start to get the impression that back in the old days, when stuff had lots of colors and lots of edges, then, that was the stuff that wasn't right. That stuff was the wrong version. You kind of start to feel you're pure about stuff.

You're lying there—it's morning, it's afternoon, it's getting dark out. Ten hours, maybe, twelve, fourteen, you're thinking about things like, pure.

I feel sorry for the people who come over. Shaun, Shaun, look at this, look who's coming to see you. Say hello Shaun when someone comes to see you.

Sometimes my brother comes by and he's got on this bright blue sweater. I'd say, "Oh, bright blue." I'd have this little shock from it.

My dad, this look on his face—I remember this look from before and it was only ever there, this one look, when my mom played piano for us.

"Shaun, come hear Mom play." My mom sits down at the piano. She plays a few things that I used to like hearing, that would calm me down.

"Play something beautiful," my dad says. "Play something smooth."

I put my hands on my ears. I won't hear it. I don't want it gliding like before. I say, "Put in some edges."

Then my mom will play something new, something sharper and harder or something—different from her old smooth stuff that sounded like gliding.

Everything was soft, before, everything was smooth—my mom at the piano, my dad in the doorway or in a chair, looking at her, her hands on the piano all gliding—everything, everyone, gliding around, like you're a really good skater. On a pond of perfect ice. And all these other skaters are out there with you and no one ever falls or bangs into you.

With this new stuff, I'd be listening to my mom, and I'd be *jolted*. It would feel like the air I was in was getting chopped at. I'd want it to keep on going like that.

I'd get interested. "Oh, hey, notes of music, they have edges."

I'm not turning into a druggie. I'm only on Tylenol, then one or two hits of the smooth stuff sometimes, not that often, twice a day. I walk around. I'm back in school. I can handle it. I've been doing my homework. But all along I keep saying to myself, "The son of the bitch broke my knee." That was one edge that stayed with me. I'd say, "Go tell Davey Peete I'm coming to his house tonight with a baseball bat."

inside

THERE WASN'T ANYTHING there that wasn't there before.
Nothing bad would happen if you went inside. You could
know things that other people didn't know about. There was
a room. There was a piano. There was a silver wall of mirrors.
There was a floor. There was a railing. But you never say railing. You have to say, "It's a bar."

The boy ballerinas put slippers on. Then they put long
noses on. They take out long noses from a box. They put on the
long noses. They look at the silver wall of the mirrors.

They put the long noses on their face where a nose is supposed to be and then they jump up and down at the bar and
take off the noses and put them sticking out from in between
their legs.

"We are Petrouchka! We are Petrouchka!" You would think
it wasn't a piano that was playing. It was just like a drum. Or a
drum and piano put together. It was Russian. You could tell
how some of the parts of the music were like, if you looked in
a kaleidoscope and there were tiny parts of pictures all in little
pieces, all falling apart, all bright colors. Some parts would
remind you of pictures in books of Russians and how if you're
a Russian you have to wear a fur hat. I don't know why you
would think of the fur hats from the music but you would.
Some parts were having a fight with some other parts and when
the music was over you would feel mad because you would
want it to start again. Some other Russian music is pretty like
in a fairy tale and everyone wears jewels but not this kind. This
kind is big and strong. It's for your blood and your bones and
your muscles. It makes you come to life if you are a puppet.

Sometimes it would be fun to be Petrouchka and sometimes it would not be fun. Things would never look good for
him, for what he wanted.

He was not handsome. He wasn't cute. He wasn't good-
looking at all, not when he was a puppet and not when he was
a boy. His hair stuck up on his head and he never combed it.
His ears stuck out. He had funny legs that were short. He
never smiled. He didn't have any friends. He stuck out his
tongue at people, even if all they said was, "How are you
today?" He was mad all the time. So everyone thought he was
bad. He told lies. He was always getting in trouble. He didn't
learn for a long time how you can be mad but you can have a
teacher and you can jump and do some steps and then the
mad is not a bad thing.

Petrouchka is what you call it when Pinocchio isn't in a car-
toon from Walt Disney. It's when Pinocchio lived in Russia.
First, there was Pinocchio in Russia, and then he swam to
America inside a whale. When he got here, a curse was on him.
They said to him in America, "Now we will make you famous
in a cartoon for babies."

Then the boy ballerinas threw away their noses and the
noses flew through the air like boomerangs, except they
didn't come back. They let go of holding the bar.

Before, at the bar, they were just like puppets. You would
really think how someone (that you couldn't see) had strings in
their hand and at the end of the strings were the boy ballerinas. Up, down. Up, down. Up, down. Turn your foot. Plee-ay!
Plee-ay! Put the heels of your feet so they are touching.
Straight lines! Put your feet in a т, upside down. Put one foot
in front of the other sideways so the toes of the foot in the front
touch the heel of the foot in the back.

How can you do this and not fall over? The boy ballerinas
do not have legs and feet of rubber. They have bones and skin,

like people. It does not seem right to be holding your feet in this way.

So Nibora went inside. She wanted to see what they were doing with their feet. It seemed to Nibora that it was just like, when someone is deaf, they have to talk to you in sign. Nibora's class at school used to have a deaf girl. Nibora learned from the deaf girl how to say, "Everyone in this school is a jerk, except you and me." She also learned, "friend," and, "I wish I could call you on the phone." The deaf girl moved away to a school where everyone was deaf. Her name was Haras. That was Sarah, backward. You sign with your fingers and this was with your feet. But it was all the same thing. It was all a way to be talking. The queen of the boy ballerinas wasn't really like a queen. Lots of days, she was in a bad mood. She wasn't quiet. She said swear words. She would never be polite like a beautiful ballerina and make you happy that you could see her. She could talk to you, though.

"Nothing bad will happen to you if you come in here," said the lady. She was at the piano. The music was playing. Nibora was still the kind of person who would rather be outside of things looking in, but sometimes, she could also be the kind of person who could go inside. The lady did not hold out her hand to Nibora but Nibora got the feeling she was. The lady said, "Can you do things with your feet?"

"One time I broke some people's coffee table," said Nibora.

"Nothing is here to break except the air," said the lady, and Nibora said, "Air can't get broken," and the lady said, "Yes it can. You can come inside all the time. I will show you some things to do. But if you give my boys any more candy, I will come after you and I will cut off your tail."

"I don't have a tail. I'm a girl," said Nibora.

"You are a little silver monkey," said the lady.

"No, I am a girl," said Nibora.

"Look at us! Look at us!" The boy ballerinas were moving their feet, all the same, all together. They turned their feet in some ways that, it did not seem to Nibora that this would feel good.

"Does it hurt to be dancing like this?" said Nibora, and the boy ballerinas said, "You have to get used to it. You have to learn," and Nibora said, *"Learn."*

They were glad to break off from the strings. The strings got broken when they threw away their noses. That was how it worked. "We can jump up on chairs! We can jump on top of a house!" That was what they were saying when they didn't have on the strings.

This is the story of Petrouchka. First he was a puppet. He thought it was a good thing to be. Then he was a boy. Then his nose grew. Then he jumped away from the bar. Then a beautiful ballerina went by. He said to her, "I am Petrouchka. I am brave and clever and I love you." But the beautiful ballerina couldn't stay. She could only visit. Anyway it could never work out.

There were some gods that lived in the clouds. One day they came down to the earth.

They said, "No one can love Petrouchka because all he is is a stupid marionette." They put a curse on the beautiful ballerina. They said, "From now on you will only be able to dance like a ballerina once a year. For the rest of the year you must never try to dance like a ballerina or we will cut off your legs."

So the ballerina could only dance once a year. She was sad and mad, put together. She didn't think she was beautiful. She would say, "I'm not beautiful. I'm just an old cow."

But there never can be a curse from a god that is simple, so there had to be another part of the curse. It was, the beautiful ballerina had to tell Petrouchka, "When you tell me you love me, I laugh at you, like you're a clown." But you could tell that the ballerina knew it was a curse. It wasn't how she would feel if the sky didn't have any gods.

Soon, Petrouchka could see that he was going to die. He wished he stayed a puppet. You can't be dead, if you are. But if he stayed a puppet he would be wood. He would not have a heart. You could see he got a heart from how he looks at the beautiful ballerina. But it has to be broken. First, it has to start beating inside his chest. Then it breaks and then he dies.

But he remembered that if someone is dead, they can't ever get to see the beautiful ballerina. This is why someone would want to not be dead, even if it was only for one day. This is how it goes. It never changes. Pretty soon, it will be the day of the year that the beautiful ballerina is going to come, and dance like a ballerina.

They are going to see her. It has to be in springtime. You would not think that Russia would get a springtime like here. But they do. They don't just have snow and fur hats. They even get an Easter. They get rain, too, and thunder.

The boy ballerinas could get up again from being dead. There was a village where Petrouchka lived. There was a little house with a roof. They climbed up on the roof. Then they were closer to where there wasn't anything else, just the air. No one else can climb like this on roofs except the ones who had a teacher and could learn.

The music was playing. Piano music and drums and pictures all broken up in little pieces and fur hats and fighting and being strong. And then the thunder would come.

So they got up from being dead and they went up on the roof and they held out their arms and they could go into the air.

They knew what to say. They talked with their feet and their legs and their arms.

They said, "Look at us! We are Petrouchka! We are Petrouchka! We're not dead! Ha ha ha! Ha ha! We're not dead!"

Then the music was faster and harder and it was like the weather. It was a storm. It was thunder and there were some way down deep piano sounds like from a barrel.

It was like when someone was asleep and there was a dream, when somebody talked or something was in it, you couldn't have any lies. One day when Nibora was just looking inside from the doorway she started talking to the lady at the piano. She asked her a question. She asked her, "Do you ever tell lies?"

"Only when I am awake," said the lady.

And Nibora asked the boy ballerinas too. "Do you tell lies?"

They said, "Only when we are not dancing."

So you can only have lies if someone wasn't asleep or not dancing. There could not be any lies if it was dreaming or dancing. This is because when you are asleep and having dreams, dreams only can have real things, not make-believe, and that is what it is like when you are dancing.

Well that was the same thing with the music after Petrouchka wasn't dead anymore.

When it was like thunder, it was like when thunder crashes in the sky. But first, there was rumbling that was like, when it was rumbling, you could hear it like your ears were inside of a barrel. The rumbling was far away but it was loud. It was an invisible barrel and it was big and you didn't know you were inside it until the rumbling came. It wasn't scary. It was deep. It was way inside you like where your heart is.

The thunder after the rumbling, when it was crashing, went into your regular ears, but not the rumbling.

You can never explain this right, in just words, but dreaming can't have lies, and then, music rumbles like outside of a barrel. You could explain it better with dancing. But you have to listen to what the music is like with some other ears. There would have to be two extra ears that you would have, for inside of the barrel.

Was getting extra ears like when Petrouchka would get a long nose? Nibora would think about that, but probably they were different things. Nibora did not want a long nose. It would get in her way.

The lady stopped playing. It was the end of the story. The boy ballerinas fell down to the floor. They said, "Look at us now! We can fall down like bowling pins!"

You could smell it how they sweated. Their hair was all wet. Their faces looked like they were crying. But they were happy. Nibora said to the lady, "How many ears do you have?"

"About a hundred," said the lady.

"I have four," said Nibora, and the lady said, "You little silver monkey, do you want to be Petrouchka, too?"

Nibora didn't know about that because Petrouchka is a boy. So Nibora said, "Do you have some other stories?"

And the lady said, "Come back inside here tomorrow, and we shall see."

boy one

THE STUDIO WAS WEIRD with the mirrors all covered as if someone had died. For the first time ever, it was weird to go in there.

She had wanted the mirrors covered. She said she knew what she was doing. "I am going to make you see what it's like when someone is at the edge of a big, white hole. Do you see what it can be like when all the world is a great white hole, top and bottom?"

"Mrs. Kamsky, this is not the world. It's your studio."

"I am trying to imagine that perhaps you are not as limited as you seem to want me to think," she said. "I am trying to convince myself that talking to you this way is not spitting into the wind. Lisette and I are trying to show you what it is like to be a dancer at the edge of the whiteness, where you think you are going to fall. Or where you think, if you are falling into this whiteness, you will fall forever, you will not know what to do. You do not seem to believe me that a dancer would understand what to do, and please don't step on the monkey. Please don't trip over the monkey," she said, because the monkey kept running around and hopping around and if you tried to control it or tell it what to do, it came over and bit your wrist. We had to just ignore the monkey.

This was my last few months with Mrs. Kamsky as my teacher. I was the oldest one she had. I was almost eighteen. I'd started out taking class with her when I was eleven. When I was eleven, we didn't call it ballet. We called it, "taking class."

"You're Boy One," she says, to me. "What you do, the others will notice."

157

"Okay then, it's not just your same old studio. It's different now. Now it's the whole big white world."

I played football. I went straight on the varsity squad as a freshman, as starting quarterback, actually, and not just because my dad's the coach. Mrs. Kamsky had resigned herself to this: someone had told her that the primary function of a football team is to always protect the quarterback from harm, like those guys came on the field with me like guardian angels. Mrs. Kamsky would not have known an end zone from, say, a zip code zone.

I helped myself out by explaining to her that a quarterback, compared to a football team, is like a principal dancer compared to just everyone else, with some soloists thrown in on both sides. She was willing to concede that the training might be useful to me. She moaned and groaned about it. She'd say, "You want to wear cleats, you should tap-dance," but she felt that it was a good idea to try making compromises with my father, on the theory that, if I kept him off my back while I still lived at home and went to school, he'd stay off it later on. Besides being the coach, he was head of our high school's athletic department.

But it wasn't the sort of thing where she or Margaret would ever come watch me play. Like I always tried to tell them, a move is a move, and you can learn some really good ones on the field.

I hadn't gotten around yet to telling my dad that when I move to San Francisco next summer, I'm not going to college. I am going to dance there. I want to put this off as long as possible, or, I will ask my mom to do it for me. This isn't being cowardly. This is being practical. Or maybe I'd get Mrs. Kamsky to do it, or Margaret, or Lisette. Or maybe I'd just go and keep quiet about it.

Every time I go to the studio now, it's a little closer to the point where she won't be my teacher anymore. Sometimes this is like walking up a cliff with a blindfold on, and when you get to the top, the wind will blow you over, and crash you down onto some rocks. Sometimes, I'd be all revved up, like a little kid that can't stand waiting for his Christmas presents.

Or I was just like a kite, in the instant when it knows that the string it's attached to has broken off, and it's two hundred feet into the air, and a good stiff breeze is up there, and it's feeling really good about everything in general, and it's feeling completely delirious.

ALL COVERED UP like that, the mirrors became something so different. They were covered with white bed sheets. There must have been six or seven sheets up there, tacked up, with the thumbtacks white, too, and you could tell that it was Margaret who had put them there because the tacks were in perfect rows.

They got some folding chairs from somewhere. The chairs were against the back wall.

The people who Mrs. Kamsky invited to the studio tonight besides us, and not counting Margaret, were: Toby Mullins, who was back from New York for a couple of days, and who really looked like hell, and Toby's mother and father, and this lady we knew from down the street, this Italian, Mrs. Gavoni, who smelled like flowery talcum powder, and the monkey and the lady who went with her, and the new kid, Dave Peete, who I was really surprised to see. The lady who went with the monkey was maybe forty or fifty—this muscular-looking lady. From the way she looked around and kept close to the monkey, she gave the impression she was a bodyguard, like she had a gun at her hip or something; she could have been a cop, a plainclothes policewoman, although she was dressed very normally, like the Italian lady and Margaret and Toby's mom, in good dresses.

These were the ones who had places, besides Margaret and Mrs. Kamsky, in the chairs. Mrs. Kamsky was wearing the same old ordinary things she always wore, which I felt was okay, since, if she had tried to fix herself up, or if she put on an ordinary dress or something, she might've looked too much like a stranger.

It was bizarre to me that Toby Mullins, sitting beside his father, was holding his father's hand. I couldn't stop looking at the way that Toby Mullins and his father were holding hands.

Toby's mom had just walked over to the piano. She sat down on the bench. She folded her hands together at the edge of the keys. There weren't any music sheets out. Mr. Bird from school was sitting on the other side of Mr. Mullins. I kept looking at his big bald head. When I first started coming to Mrs. Kamsky, Mr. Bird hung around all the time, I didn't know yet he was a teacher. He had looked, to me, like Goliath, coming and going and ducking low in Mrs. Kamsky's low doorways. I tried to imagine what it felt like to Toby Mullins to be practically a grownup, and sit there and hold hands with his father.

The perfumey smell of the Italian lady was so thick, it felt like there must have been flowers all over the room, but there weren't any flowers. There were only the covered mirrors, and the barre, same as always, and the old familiar white walls that looked so suddenly different, and the folding chairs, and the invited guests who sat in them, and the piano, the same old piano, unaltered.

At the back of the studio, either sitting on the floor with their legs tucked out of the way, or standing up against the wall, there were also the guests who had not been invited—well, not officially. As soon as the word had gotten out that Lisette was dancing tonight, everyone in the valley, who the word had gotten out to, they were here: they had decided right away to drop whatever they were doing. There were also some pupils of other teachers, and teachers themselves, four or five of them. You could tell in one second which people were the dancing teachers. I recognized a few of them—they'd been here before for visits with Mrs. Kamsky. One way or another I felt like all the people on the sidelines over there had faces that were familiar to me.

I didn't know that Toby Mullins's mom could play the piano. I wondered if, seeing as how she played the piano, Mrs. Mullins had a piano at home. I wondered what it would be like to be the kind of person whose mom had a piano in their living room. I couldn't imagine what this would be like. It always would seem to me that people who had pianos in their houses were only on TV or in the movies. I didn't know that much personally about Toby, except that, sure, I knew about everything going on in his career, I kind of paid attention to it: and my overall feeling was that, sooner or later, I'd end up as a principal dancer, and he wouldn't, or, if he did, and then, so did I, and you compared us, I'd probably be able to like blow him right out of the water, and it wouldn't be just only by how I jump. I'd say, "Sorry, Toby, but you never played football."

Or maybe that's not going to be the way it works out for me at all. Sometimes when I think about "going away to San Francisco," I can't picture at all what might be waiting there for me. All I can picture is the airplane, with me strapped into a seat, landing on a runway that isn't long enough, and the pilot would say, "hold on now, folks, because everyone's going to die," and then we'd glide off the edge of America like a big silver eagle made of tin.

I'd be thinking, "Oh, what a great piece of luck." We'd go into the ocean, and I'd be sitting there feeling lucky.

Just when you thought it couldn't get any quieter, with all these people in here, it got quieter. I don't know what I expected. If anyone asked me what I think the basic difference is between football and dancing, I would say that, in football, there's more clothes: you get to wear a helmet, and you get to pad yourself. You don't have to go out there in just practically your skin. And if things go wrong, you can always say, even if it pisses off certain people, "it's just a game."

I had never seen Lisette dance. It was one thing to be weirded all out from looking at the mirrors, from seeing white sheets where I was used to always seeing my own reflection. It was something completely different to be worried like this about Lisette.

It wasn't like this was a public thing in a theater with strangers in the seats. It was only Mrs. Kamsky's same old studio. But that kind of thing didn't matter. All of my life since I was eleven years old, there had been in this studio, like a ghost—like those sheets on the mirrors, but invisible—there had always been Lisette. When you went out on the floor for adagio, your arms would learn first to hold the air. And your arms would learn second to hold Lisette, an imaginary, phantom Lisette, which was a huge relief, compared with Mrs. Kamsky. Every boy who ever studied with Mrs. Kamsky had learned to do lifts by picking up Mrs. Kamsky.

She must have kept putting on weight for this reason. She would stand there, and you had to learn some complicated things with your hands, on account of her arthritic hips. So we learned things to do with our hands that the dancers of other teachers might not know. If you could lift Mrs. Kamsky off the floor by even three inches, then, no one could ever throw a partner at you who you wouldn't be able to handle.

I guess I expected that, when I actually saw Lisette dancing, I would only come away from it disappointed. The most I could get my hopes up for would be, she didn't go out there and try to make everyone feel sorry for her. I very strongly

felt that, if she came out here, and she was sloppy and sentimental, like, "I'm this washed-up old cow and the only reason I'm dancing tonight is, Mrs. Kamsky said I have to,"
which was totally, completely true—well, if that was the way
she did it, it wouldn't be right. It did not seem possible to me
that seeing her dancing, in real life, might be better than
what I'd always imagined. So I was really hit over the head
with it when she came in. She wore old white toe shoes,
white tights, a white leotard, and a gray, practice-style skirt,
the kind that goes down to the knees, light and silky.

Or maybe the skirt was light blue. Her arms were bare.
She wore no makeup. Her hair was pulled back in a bun.
Every muscle she had, every inch of herself, she was in total
control of it.

She walked directly to the center of the floor, positioned
herself with her face turned away from the mirrors, and
started dancing.

Mrs. Mullins was a little bit late coming in on the piano,
but that was okay, too. It gave you some time to get used to
the fact that the ballerina out there was Lisette, not a phantom. Toby Mullins and his father let go of holding hands. Mr.
Bird put his hands together in front of his chest and sat there
like that, unembarrassed. He held his hands together the way
kids play, "Here is the church, here is the steeple."

Someone had turned off half of the overhead track lights.
There was one track of lights on Lisette. Someone must
have changed the bulbs earlier to a brighter wattage. The way
the lights were pointed, and with the second track turned
off, Lisette cast no shadows. We could see that the light she
was in was moonlight, but she wasn't any sleepwalker out
there. She was wide awake. You forgot that the mirrors were
covered with the whiteness. You just thought they were normal, now.

I don't know how long she danced. It could have lasted
fifteen minutes; it could have been a lot longer. I don't even
know what music Mrs. Mullins was playing. I felt like my ears
had been shut off, in some kind of weird compression, like
we were up in a plane or something, like the sheets on the
mirrors were fog banks.

There is a step called pas de bourrée which basically, only
a ballerina can do. It means that you're walking while up on
your toes, or up on the edges of your toenails, I guess. When
they do it, especially for like a hundred yards or something, it
works on your eyes a strange way. It's like they're gliding away
from you on toes that turned into, in fact, two points on a pair
of scissors, with both points equally sharp. You have to step on
your feet like this as lightly, as airily, as if your body was as
light as empty clothes. You have to make it look like you had
learned to do this step very naturally, but you never would
have learned it from someone on earth. You had to learn how
to do it from aliens, faraway aliens, who had invented it a long
time ago as a method to go walking in space.

This was the way Lisette went out of the studio when she
finished dancing.

Someone had pushed open the door that led into Mrs.
Kamsky's kitchen. Lisette did not return to take a bow.

It was a good thing that Mrs. Mullins started playing something else on the piano. She played very quietly, and it gave
everyone a reason to keep sitting there a little longer, and give
our hearts the chance to start beating again in normal ways.

I wondered, when my last day comes before I leave Mrs.
Kamsky, will Lisette come back here again and dance like
that for me?

She was just like an alien. She went out very slowly. She
glided away from us smoothly on her points, with her head
tucked down low, with her arms curved out in front of her

from the waist, and with her hands not touching each other. Maybe it was supposed to look as if she carried some kind of a bundle, or maybe it was supposed to look as if this is how, when you're walking in a world full of whiteness, you hold the air.

davey

I HAD THIS DREAM the night after I went to see Lisette.

It was a nightmare. I turned into metal. The first thing that went was my feet. They were like these two iron feet. Then my legs went totally aluminum like a tube on a vacuum cleaner, first one then the other, these two leg-wide aluminum tubes. Then my head was not a head anymore; it was a tin can, like I still had my own hair and my own face but it was hair and a face on a can. Then from the neck down it was like a tin barrel was on me, and I was way inside this tin barrel.

No one told me about how I'd be stuck like that, with having her make me go metal. In the dream she didn't look like the same Lisette that had danced here. The night she danced here she looked like a dream, but in my dream she just looked like this thirty year old or something, no big deal, like someone you'd see at the grocery store, totally married, like she goes out of the house and doesn't look in a mirror to see what she looks like. I was trying to walk around but my feet were these bricks made of iron. I knocked on my ribs and there were these tinny echoes. I was like, if I could lift up one leg I could kick in a wall. I was never so glad to wake up like I was when I woke up from that dream.

Ah, says Mrs. Kamsky, perhaps it was very upsetting for you to be sent to her hotel room to let her look at you as a dancer, and then perhaps you had a desire, as you might admit so yourself, if you would think about this fully, to make love to her. You felt some desire and so you went home and dreamed you are shall we say incompetent. Is this what you are trying to tell me?

No fucking way!

Ah, but a hotel room, a young boy, a beautiful woman, do not be so prudish with me, as it would seem to make sense for you to have these feelings.

It was a *dream*. She's too old. I wasn't nervous. It was just, this hotel room. You said to make it look like it wasn't the first time I ever was in one so I didn't, I looked like I go in them all the time.

I go in and I say to her, Mrs. Kamsky said I had to come and see you. She's got on these normal clothes: a T-shirt, plain white, and these baggy pants like they wear in those cults, those Hare Krishnas or something, but black, not orange. I thought she had casts on her feet, these hard plastic casts like you can walk around in them but they're casts.

I say, it's pretty cool how you can have casts now that they don't make with plaster like in the old days. She says, Davey, these are my slippers.

She is sensitive about her feet, says Mrs. Kamsky. Let us not think about you lifting one leg like a dog and deciding to be kicking a hole in a wall. Let us think about when you walked in. When she looked at you did she look at you as one would look at a picture on a wall that was a small one, that you don't have to step back from, to be able to see it altogether?

She stepped back like I was a really big picture. But all she said was a few basic things. She started it off, and she said that she was leaving all the rest of it to you. You're supposed to be filling in the blanks, and she said to tell you, there's this guy that works with metals and it's in a metalworker's shop, but I bet you she wouldn't mind it if we switched it around.

When you walked into her hotel room, did you look like a boy who makes trouble?

No, I looked great. What's the matter with her feet?

Oh, nothing that isn't normal. Did you show her what it was like for you to watch her dancing? Did you tell her the truth? Did you stand there like a wall, or did you do the right thing, and tell her, Lisette, when I saw you dance the other night at Mrs. Kamsky's, my heart began to beat a different way, I was perhaps a little tiny bit less of a barbarian from the state of my usual self, plus, you looked like a very good dream?

Yeah, I did, I did.

I am trying to picture this. Her suitcases are packed?

They're on the bed. They're sitting on the bed. She's looking at the time because she's worried about missing her plane.

Her hair is loose today?

Yeah, loose, but don't be calling me a barbarian.

Perhaps I will not be able to any longer when you have learned to do things with lifting your legs besides kicking and causing damages and saying fuck like you are someone with no graces. Perhaps we can think about what she said to you. She tells you, ah, you are a lucky, lucky boy to be someone we are taking an interest in.

No, she says she feels sorry for me, and in a couple of years, I am going to feel like, my whole life is like a total waste of time, and I tell her it was kind of getting wasted anyway. Then she tells me how there's this new thing and this thing is going on in a metalworker's shop.

A shop? A metalworker?

That's what she said. But we didn't have much time. She had to get out to the airport, she's got like two kids out there waiting for her to come home, so I say, come on, Lisette, we need to speed this up, could it be woodworking, could it be carpenters, which I'd be better off picturing? And she says, I don't give a damn what you picture, Davey, you can picture whatever you want, but this is my hotel room, and this is my dance, and it's a metalworker's shop. It's this shop for one. It's this guy like, he's a welder or something, he's in this shop. He makes stuff. I don't know what stuff. Metal stuff. Tin stuff. She kept saying to me, tin, tin, tin. How should I know how come?

Ah, if this is so, we can see what is the source of your dream. I would have thought you dreamed of yourself as a metal man because of the way you moved your body when she looked at you.

I moved okay, I was pretty flexible like you said. You said I had to show her I could stand there like a dancer so I did.

And as for kicking, was there something for you to kick?

The air, Mrs. Kamsky. You said, kick like I can bust up the air, so I did.

But I don't believe I know why she would say that, tin. I am trying to understand this metal. I don't believe I know myself what a metal shop looks like. Maybe we should ask Margaret to take you out in the car, and go and look at one. I'm sure she could find you one to go and look at.

Mrs. Kamsky, who cares? The guy's out there by himself. There's no real machines. He's at work in there, but it's a totally bare stage. Go along with me. What does it matter what's in my head? Let's say it's a woodworking shop. She won't know, she can write it in the program as metal.

I've promised that I will fill in the blanks here. You and Lisette have given me many more blanks to concern myself with than you could possibly imagine. I do not know the reason for this welder. But this is what I'm trying to do. You will have to be patient with me. You come here to tell me what happened, and you are saying to me, tin, metal, more tin. This is not what I expected. Did she play you some music?

She said she would leave that to you. She said to tell you, I don't give a damn what country.

Ah, then, perhaps we will have something to begin with after all that perhaps I can try to understand. Did she tell you she believes I am correct in thinking you are someone with a future in dancing?

She said you're never correct about anything but that doesn't mean I shouldn't listen to you. Play some music! Play the piano stuff that goes really fast. The choppy guy, you know what I'm talking about?

We will wait a little longer for the choppy guy. Do you tell me he is choppy because you see his name on the music sheet and this is how you think to pronounce it?

I said choppy because that's what you look like when you play him. You look like you're chopping the keys.

Is that what should go on in the shop of this tin man? Chop chop chop all day long?

He would be doing stuff.

But you are telling me that you cannot get it into your mind to picture yourself in any other shop but a wood one. This is the problem we are speaking about.

I guess I got this block about it. But that's how I already started thinking about it. Now I'm ready to show you the steps. Can I show you the steps now, please?

I wonder if perhaps you might wait for that for another moment. Perhaps you might consider the effect you would have. You would be dancing with a head full of wood. Is that, do you think, what you should show me? A dance of a block-head? Am I filling in a thing that has no brain?

It already has a brain, Mrs. Kamsky. It has a really good one, I could tell. When she was saying to me, Davey, we're making up this new dance and you're playing this guy who works with metal, she was *into* it. She was kind of telling me that this was something she thought about, like kind of deep. I said to her, Lisette, are you crying?

Ah, she looked at you trying to dance and began to cry?

No, it wasn't on account of me.

She was sentimental about this metal man?

Yeah, sentimental, but she wasn't crying like, with tears, and she wasn't all gushy, she was totally focused.

We will have to see about this deepness, this focus, this thinking. I must get used to the idea that there are things about Lisette I do not know. But let us consider this shop. Does a wood shop have grease all over the floor, grease and oil, absolutely everywhere?

Yeah, sure, there's grease.

But I would think there would be, in a wood shop, which of course you would be used to, oh, very much less of it. I would expect to see sawdust packed down on the floor. Sawdust, and shavings of wood. I would ask myself the question if a boy at work in a metal shop would walk across the floor the same way as a boy among shavings and sawdust.

Yeah, he would. Anyway in the metal shop, he'd be used to it.

But I wonder if the floor in a metal shop would be unusually slippery. I would also think, it must be made of cement.

Mrs. Kamsky, in a wood shop, there's nails all over the floor. Everybody has boots on, but there's junk, there's stuff that could impale you if you stepped on it.

I wonder if impale is quite the point here. Perhaps you are a little tiny bit forgetting that you are a beginner. There are many things for you to be thinking about. Perhaps the little thing you should be doing here is simply walking around for a minute without tripping and falling and bumping into things, and slipping on a puddle of oil that perhaps had not been there the day before.

Mrs. Kamsky, if you're trying to invent a new dance here, let me tell you, it's turning out to be totally boring.

But I wonder if perhaps the temperature of a metal shop would differ by many degrees from a wood shop.

It would be hotter. I would probably sweat more. But that wouldn't make a big difference.

I see. I wonder if perhaps the same would apply to how it sounds.

It would have to be noisy. But all shops, it doesn't matter which kind, they're all noisy.

Then perhaps you'll want to show us how nice it would look to be able not to fall on such a slippery floor, which no one but a dancer would dare to walk on. First, you will show us that you are a dancer. This is the way it begins, with every dance. Perhaps slowly, after that, you will begin to get it into your head where you are.

Can I dance now? I'm edgy.

Go home now. We will not dance today. Come and see me again, perhaps soon, when you are willing to let me teach you something you don't know. Come and see me when you are thinking of other things besides edgy and wood.

So I went home and I was like, no way can I keep dealing with crazy dreams and I couldn't think of what else to do except call up my old gramma.

She's like ninety. She's in a nursing home but they can put up the phone to her ear.

Gramma, help me out, and she says, okay, on account of how I was always the one she liked best of my brothers and even her own kids, and she would pretty much always take my side about things no matter what, even if it was just to piss off my dad. She's my dad's mother. Every single relative my gramma ever had except for me was in the construction business.

I get her on the phone. I tell her, you need to stop praying for me to Saint Joseph.

But she says, like I didn't know this fact my whole life, Saint Joseph the father of Jesus is the patron saint of our family and of carpenters everywhere throughout the world. This is the one who I pray to, every day, my whole life, she says, and I tell her, gramma, it's not working out for me so good that way because, I'm not a carpenter.

I say, I'm a metalworker, and she says, who is this? Is this Davey?

Yeah, it's Davey, and she says, there's no saint I ever heard of for just metal, but here is what I'll do for you. I won't be praying to him for you as a carpenter. I'll be praying to him for you as Jesus's father, do you think that would help? I say, yeah, start right now. I think it would, I think it would.

class

YOU CAN CALL IT whatever you like, but here is what we're doing with you today. Admit what's going on here. You have got to admit to us that you are willing to talk with us about the way that things between us, lately, have deteriorated.

It is not enough that you tell us you are sorry for failing to pay to us the sort of attention that we had expected you to pay.

This is what you can't say. You can't say, oh, I'm sorry for my part in the way that things between us got so bad, but my hips having been giving me trouble, it's very much both of them now, there are many different things going wrong, and look at me, I am getting, quite suddenly, so much older.

In other words, don't be coming over to the barre like this and looking at yourself in the mirror and saying, oh, in place of myself, there's poor old Hecuba, because we found out who that is. Mrs. Kamsky, we apologize here for being overly realistic with you, but you're not that bad off, you know, and this is not, like, the Trojan war. You need to stop saying this kind of thing to us, because it frightens us, and look what happened to Hecuba. We got Margaret to go look it up. She went to the library. The Greeks killed her family. The Greeks burned down Troy. Everything she used to have, the Greeks wrecked. Don't be bringing up this stuff with us. You're not Hecuba. You've got stuff. Hecuba was totally tragic, and then she turned into a dog.

Plus Margaret called up Lisette and found out, there's no Troy in this new dance. There's a metalworker and he's American, there's no Troy, is what Lisette told Margaret.

And you can't be saying it's a dance for just one, we can't be in it, when we tell you how much it bothers us that you and Lisette are making up a new dance for only one.

We know about the new dance. We want to be in it. We don't care what you tell us to do. We'll be anything you want. Make us shadows. We'll be fire, flames of fire, we'll be the glows off burning rods. We'll be tongs, hammers, rods, tin, a hunk of iron, whatever. We'll be machines. We'll act like our bodies are furnaces.

Did Margaret tell you already that she wants you to put in a personal nursemaid or something, or did she leave that to us?

Oh, she left it to us. We just ran into her ten minutes ago outside in the street, and she said, when the right moment comes up, ask her to put in a nursemaid, or you could call it a personal attendant.

You will have to take care of that idea on your own. We know that there will have to be a ballerina in the dance. Even if there is no ballerina, if the whole thing's a dance for guys, there will be a ballerina. There will be an idea. There will have to be some light in the dance, and the light will come in like light of the moon, and we'd be standing there going, oh, there's Lisette.

You will have to decide if someone like this would need a nursemaid, like the one for Juliet, but not so fat, and not so cowardly.

Margaret told us that's what we have to call her now, instead of "health care aide." Margaret said, "Call me a nurse-maid because that's what you call it in all the famous stories."

Probably, the best thing to do about this, if Margaret tries to force you to put a nursemaid in, like, she'll go on strike or something, then, you should tell her, that's something that Lisette and I will be saving for another new dance, perhaps our next one. Say, I promise that one day soon, I'll invent a new dance about Margaret.

This is how it is. It could go either way if you and Lisette make a dance later on to put us into.

We wonder if perhaps it makes you worried and unhappy that we don't completely believe you when you say you'll make others, that really, this is only a practice, there'll be others later on.

We are sorry if it crosses your mind that we do not fully trust you.

There is no one to guard you or help you. We locked both studio doors, and the doors of your house are locked, too. No one will bother us at this time of the day, and the monkey's in school, and Margaret, you know, would never take your side if it was us who opposed you.

Perhaps this might be making you a little nervous and lonely.

We wouldn't call it a revolt. "Revolt" would be boring. We would only be stomping around and ganging up on you. We would ask you to consider the possibility that, we can sometimes engage in being interesting. We can sometimes do things that may surprise you.

What we're doing here is, you can call it, we're taking you hostage, or you can call it, a mutiny.

Do you see what we are saying? Look at what we're showing you. If this were any other country, you would be challenged to a duel. We are terrorists, or mutineers.

We are not in the mood today to stand back and allow you to make fun of us. We did not say, we are mutants. We said, mutineers. On a ship, Mrs. Kamsky, a big ship.

Try to imagine that the piano is a ship. Try to remember that the number of people on board who would help you out is just about zero.

Now, this thing in our hands that we're dragging along the deck, it's a plank. We just got done tearing it out of the wall.

Look over at the mirrors, at the barre. Do you see that a part of the barre is missing? That's because we've turned it into a plank.

We're putting it on top of the piano. We're serious. We are not playing Peter Pan pirates here, either.

Let's see what we'll do. Let's see if we'll rescue you at like, the last minute. Or let's see if we feel like throwing you today to the sharks. Or let's see if, perhaps, we let you off the hook about this, for now, and then we'll go after Davey instead.

Okay, we promise to try hard to lay off Davey.

Now, get up on the plank, Mrs. Kamsky, please, because you're just about ready to start walking it.

She sees that we are not giving her a choice. She gets up from the bench.

Davey starts going over to her, not to hold onto her, but to stand there in case she started to fall, but we go, Davey, don't, she *hates* that.

We say, you have a lot to learn, Davey, and Davey goes, if she falls they'll take her in for more new parts.

She won't fall when we're watching her, she never does. We say, Davey, sit down and be quiet, and he does.

Mrs. Kamsky goes, I'll be getting on top of the piano now.

The ocean's all stormy, the waves are high, they have big whitecaps. There's white spray. Everything is grayness and whiteness. You're right at the edge of the plank. You have nothing to hold onto. Are you nervous?

She's out on the floor, she's standing there. It's like she's really on top of the piano. It's kind of windy up here, she says.

She's up there looking at us. It gets quiet. Is she showing us something new? She says, I'm showing this to Davey.

She goes, this is how you show what it is like to be ready to jump into the air. And this is what it is like when, you are ready to jump in the air, and, at the very last minute, you don't jump.

She goes, this is what it is like to want your feet to leave the ground, and they do not.

We go, is the metalworker stuck to the ground?

This is what I'm telling you, she says. His heart is too heavy.

We go, Davey, you watching this? Yeah, I'm watching.

She's up on the piano. She's saying, to Davey, this is what it feels like to be standing on the earth.

This is what it feels like to be earthbound. It feels like the wood on the top of the piano. Under the wood is where the music will come from, and Davey goes, yeah, wood, under the wood, and she goes, to us, now I will show you something you have not seen before.

She goes, you must be patient, and then she told us something else. We looked at her face. It could have seemed, if you didn't know her, that, all she was doing was standing there, but she wasn't just standing there. She was talking to us.

She closed her eyes a little bit, not completely. This look came on her face. Are you Hecuba from burned-down Troy?

Not at the moment. Do you see what I am showing you, she goes, and we go (but not Davey), oh, are you showing us what you look like when you imagine that you are watching us dance?

That is what I'm doing exactly, she goes.

We go, do you imagine that, when we jump in the air, we are better at jumping than animals, and we are better at flying than birds? She goes, flying like a bird is not that difficult.

Any old thing with two wings can fly, she goes, and she gets down from the piano. She shakes herself off. She flaps her arms, like she's shaking off drops of water, white water, white foam.

It wasn't that hard to picture her as a short white bird, this short white gull with two big wings and the head and hair and face of Mrs. Kamsky. She was looking at us with shiny eyes, like she just came back to us from flying around. She made those loud noisy screeches that seagulls make. She's looking at us. She's saying, I can tell you from personal experience, there is only one thing a bird envies, and that is, a dancer. She's shaking her head at us, saying over and over how any old thing with two wings can fly.

the hazeltons

IF WE HAD TO give a piece of advice to parents of children who start dancing, this is what we would say: a leotard is like a one-piece bathing suit with short sleeves, and it's the first thing they wear when they get started.

You must never allow the child to wear a leotard at home. This is something you will need to enforce vigorously. Don't wait till it's too late, like we did. You'll be sorry. They will take you as their hostage, emotionally. When a child wears a leotard around the house, they will get the idea that there is nothing a grown-up would refuse them. There is something about wearing a leotard that makes the child say, "I am perfect already, as I am, and the last thing I need is for my mother and father trying to improve me." Surrender. If you try to resist, you will never have a peaceful moment.

Last night after supper, in her leotard, our daughter got up and pushed back her chair and got up on the chair and stood there on tiptoes and arched up her back and laid down some rules for how things are going to be. We have to get ready right now for the future so that, when it comes, we'll know exactly what to do.

First, she'll put on her costume, on top of her leotard. She'll be getting ready in her dressing room. No one in the audience can see her between the time she starts putting on her costume and the time she comes out. It's bad luck.

Then she'll come out. She will see that we have been sitting here waiting for her. She'll take a bow and we can clap, but only a little. We must pretend that this is the first time we've ever seen her. We must sit very still and keep quiet.

Some music will play. She'll start doing some steps. Sometimes there's an extra empty space in between a few steps, before the next one gets going, but this isn't where you clap. It's where you're even more quiet than before.

We must not try to act like her family. We must try to act like everybody else. We must try to blend in with the audience.

When the music is playing, we must not move around in our seats. Only the ballerina can move. We must not tap our fingers on our knees, chew gum, poke at each other, or tap our feet on the floor. We must especially not wave our arms in the air as though we were acting the part of the conductor of the music. We must act like we are under a spell. Because of the spell, only the ballerina can be the one in the room who can move.

We must keep quiet when we see her come in. We must not clap louder than other people at the end of the steps. But if all the other people clap loud, then so can we, to blend in. We must try very hard to behave. We must try to never embarrass her.

"All ballerinas must change their names," she explains.

We will have to accept it and call her by the different name. She will have to have a name that suits a ballerina. She does not think that "Robin" is such a name. First, it's not that lively of a bird, a robin, in fact it mostly stays around on the lawn, it's very unadventurous.

"Any old thing with two wings can fly," she tells us. "It's not that big of a deal."

Second, the Robin of Batman and Robin, and the Robin of Robin Hood, are boys. These Robins are of no use to her. She is a girl.

Now we must call her Ballerina Kathleen, with an "ah" in it: Kathaleen. We must try out her new name often. It's the wrong name to pick absolutely but she's going through phases, so we don't argue with her. It's not worth the effort. "Ballerina Kathaleena is sorry that she has to be so strict with you, but it's for your own good," she tells us. We say "yes" to every one of her terms. What else could we do? It began to seem as though she'd come to us in a pod from outer space, and here she was, standing on a chair, squaring back her shoulders, looking at us with a strange bright glint in her eyes: a pure-hearted light-footed thin round monkey-faced martian, who had suddenly started speaking a language that we did not understand.

She wants us to figure out what the different positions are, so that, when we watch her at home, we'd know if she was getting them wrong. She put a chart of the positions of the feet on the front of our refrigerator, held on with her alphabet magnets from babyhood. She taped a chart of the arms on the wall of our upstairs bathroom.

We are not allowed to go to her teacher's house to watch her. Her teacher does not let in parents. We can go over there now and then and ring the front doorbell and say hello and pay for her lessons (in cash) and that is all. One time, we tried to explain to her teacher that when Robin started studying with her, and came home and showed us what she had learned, we felt as though we were suddenly living our life like someone in the movie *e.t.* (if *e.t.* had come to earth to the home in an east-coast suburb of a married professional couple). But the point of it was lost on her, as Mrs. Kamsky had not known who *e.t.* was.

mr. bird

THE OLD BALLERINA is home alone tonight, in her galley of a kitchen. I don't bother knocking. We've been friends a long time and she has always made me know that, wherever she is, or whatever room she's in, that place or that room is a home to me.

Say that there's an old Trojan soldier. At forty-four, he feels old. It's been dawning on him slowly that, more and more, his shoulders are sagging; his back hurts; his head is as heavy as a wooden block, and his eyes are always stinging, like eyes that have shed a lot of tears, and run dry. Sometimes it seems that the heart has gone out of him. Sometimes, he knocks at his own chest with his knuckles, and swears that he hears only echoes, and he wonders how hollow you can be and still keep living. "Hecuba," he says, "it's good to see you."

Hecuba is still alive. She wants to make it clear that she is not the Hecuba of Euripides, who was dragged from Troy as the slave to a corrupt Greek king. She is the Hecuba of Ovid and Virgil, beloved of Romans, not Greeks.

Hecuba bends at the waist like a woman who is old, old, old. I am standing in thin gray shadows, in her hallway. She says, "I suppose I should feel lucky that the island I've ended up on has peace and quiet."

She makes the effort to appreciate peace and quiet. It doesn't work. Parts of her are missing. Parts of her have been replaced. She understands the basic fact that for her, the whole Trojan War is in her body, like rust.

"I am rusting, and here's Aeneas," she says, for passing by her island, I had decided to make a stop.

I found her on a hillside, all wild gray hair and old bones. We two old Trojans embrace.

Her face is pale, her teeth feel loose in her mouth. Her heart is still pumping in the usual way but the blood in her veins is as cold as the salty ocean. She knows, as I do, that the dead can't speak to the living, no more than a stone on the ground will grow legs, and get up and walk about like a turtle. What's gone is gone. But sunlight falls onto the stone and heats it. Moonlight falls onto the stone; so do shadows.

It's late in the autumn, very dark and very gray, and it's raining, it's been raining like this all week, and I know that she is missing her old life, and all the people she has known, whom she will never see again.

She washes her hair at the sink. She keeps it cut short for this reason. She wishes she could keep this a secret, but she can't get into her bathtub by herself any longer, although the walls of her bathroom have new metal railings.

Raising her head from under the faucet, she bangs into it so hard, she worries that she might have broken it, or loosened it off its screws, but it's still all in there in one piece.

She checks her head for a bruise and doesn't find one. She swabs her wet hair with a towel. She shakes her head like a dog, and drops of water fall everywhere.

It was never easy being Queen of Troy but it was like childhood, like playtime, compared to what she now has to cope with: she's still alive.

Hecuba holds onto the back of a chair, for the support, and dries her hair. She finishes this, and hands me the towel. I hang it up. Each small movement of hers, each gesture, is slow, slow, slow, as though a wind-up toy were running down.

Hecuba is dancing tonight for me. She looks around with her eyes wide open, as though searching for something, which she hardly dares hope to be able to see.

She bows her head like a old woman praying. She taps one foot lightly on the floor, as a horse can be trained to tap out numbers. Tap, tap, tap, on and on, tap, tap, tap, tap, tap. She is counting her losses. I know what this is like. It takes a long time.

We listen to what it sounds like in her house. There is the rain. There is the absence of music. Oh, she says, just a while ago, she'd gone into the other room to put the stereo on. But guess who'd been in there before her. Look at the note she had left, the way a nurse for a patient with Alzheimer's would have done, when they forget the simplest things, and must have signs taped up everywhere, saying, "this is your rug," or, "this is your sofa," or, "this was always your favorite room."

The note sticks up from the rows of the phonograph albums at the beginning of the letter M. The records are alphabetical, and are largest in number in the Ms and the Bs and the Ss. Tonight, the Ms appear to have dwindled. "I should have told Margaret that going to the library and getting educated was not a part of her job description," she says.

"Dear Irene," says the note. "I just took your records of Mr. Gustav Mahler home with me. I checked up on this, and he's the only one you've got here that, he composed a kind of music that is not for dancing ballet to. Stick with the happier ones. I also want to tell you, you should never be listening to this man in this awful weather. And it's not because he was German. It's because he was insane. See you in the morning. Yours truly, Margaret (your nursemaid). P.S., if you've got company and it's Mr. Brrr, and I bet you anything he is standing there reading this right now, don't you dare send him home to get his Mahlers and let you borrow them."

"For crying out loud, I can't do anything," says Hecuba.

The old pair of sweatpants she's wearing had slipped down off her waistline, and she hitches them up and ties the strings a little tighter. She eats oatmeal for breakfast and, if she wants it sweetened, there's not one drop of sugar to be found: she has to cut up a peach or put some grapes in. For lunch, tuna from a can, like cat food. For dinner, dry white poultry, no bread, and a bowl of lettuce like food for a rabbit. For pain, ice cubes. For a great deal of it, ice cubes more often in the tub. For a snack in the afternoon, saltines from Weight Watchers and two carrots.

She picks up her shirt from the counter and slings it over her shoulder. She gives her head one more shake and turns off the kitchen light. Inside, it's nearly as gray as outdoors. She says, "I was hoping you'd bring me a quart of ice cream and I wouldn't care what flavor, as long as it had the highest fat content you can buy, and I also would have liked a box of Dunkin Donuts, glazed."

"I'm too afraid of Margaret."

"Well, I'll send the monkey to the store tomorrow, so never mind."

She pauses, straightens up a little and raises her arms. She holds out her arms in front of her, straight out, like an old cartoon of a sleepwalker. She takes a step backward and curves out her arms in front of her breasts, as though she's pulling something in, toward her heart. It's as though she is gathering air, an invisible bag filled with air. Her feet make a short, gliding gesture, as though the floor is made of ice. She does not appear to be afraid of falling over.

I do not know, I do not like to stop and wonder, what kind of a hole there would be in my life if I could not come here—if I were not the one person, in this town, this valley, this world, to be with her when she dances.

All along, it's been steadily raining, straight down.

"Aeneas," she says. "Sometimes, I am sick of being human."

I hold her hands. Fur is coming over her skin. Her hands and her feet are turning into paws. I step back, worried. "Do you want me to help you into the tub? Do you need an icing before you sleep tonight?"

"No tub."

She bends forward, as though picking something up that she had dropped—slowly, slowly, in a perfectly normal way, like any old woman who is slowly stooping over. She touches the ground with one hand then the other. She's down on all fours and I get down beside her. I remind her there is nothing I would not do for her. I touch her hair. I've been through a lot, she knows all of it: the Greeks, Dido, my friends all clutching at their hearts and falling dead, a sea god trying to drown me, a very great weight on my back, shipwrecks, and a god for a parent, because my mother, as it happens, is Venus.

Hecuba has always felt strongly that this is something which cannot be overlooked.

Once, back in Troy, she had pulled me aside and advised me. She felt that, yes, a god for a mother has its drawbacks, but there are also advantages, because I never know when she'll suddenly turn up. "Every time you look up at a cloud, the cloud could turn out to be her, although ninety-eight percent of the time, it would only be a cloud. Now don't be complaining about getting on your feet every day and going to work, even if your chest is making echoes because you haven't got a heart. You're a teacher, you're like me, you make do with the two percent of when it's not just clouds," she had told me.

After that, like it or not, I had my eyes on the two percent. I am always craning my neck and looking up carefully at clouds.

"It's not that bad to keep living," I tell her.

She's back up on her feet. "When you were dancing on stage," I ask her, "did you wear your hair in a bun?"

"Everyone did. I used to be very conventional."

All along, the sound of the rain, as it falls against her house, is as predictable as a water sprinkler. But it's a fairly windy night. Now and then, every couple of minutes or so, when the wind comes up a little harder, rain strikes at the windows with a sudden, startling clatter—it can be heard very clearly; it's a tinny, light sound, like needles shooting out of a bucket.

Hecuba has forgotten that there aren't any records in the parlor tonight to be played, and that there's nothing to listen to except the rain.

She pricks up her ears at the first sound of rising wind. Windblown rain strikes hard at the windows, pointed, quick, and sharp, like airborne needles and pins. It's raining tonight in needles and pins. It's raining tonight in pieces of silver metal.

"I'll come by tomorrow and see how you are. Can you get into bed on your own?"

"I can."

"Then good night, Irene. I'll be seeing you in my dreams."

She says, "That's what everyone tells me."

I walk backward toward the front door, on my way to get back to my ship. When I reach it, I'll wave to her from the deck. "I'm still watching you," I say. There's hardly any furniture; I know what I'm not bumping into.

She's standing there. She looks as though she's scanning the line of a horizon. She turns her head this way and that, as if watching a metronome, or a ping-pong game, if the game were played in slow motion. When the rain strikes the windows in a certain way, it sounds as though the glass is being pierced with tiny holes.

There are no cracked windows, there are no perforations, it's only rain. But she tips back her head anyway, as though outside air is rushing in, like a spray, like a spraying of air from a fountain, whitecapped and watery, and icy and sharp and salty, like the sea. And I wonder if it sounds to her ears as if many, many people are applauding her, instead of just me.

class

SHE THINKS WE MIGHT like it very much if she and Lisette make a waltz for us to begin with. A waltz? A waltz like this is ballroom dancing?

Oh, she and Lisette are fond of waltzes and there is no good reason why there shouldn't be a waltz.

We look at what she's showing us. She's sitting on the bench at the piano. She shows us "waltz." She holds out her arms in the air, tips her head. She reaches back to the keys and plays a few notes. Dah dah dah dah dah, dah dah.

It's nice but how about something more advanced? This is too basic for us.

Basic is for the dancers who are brave, she says. You want to show off? You want fancy schmancy? You want tricks? Go to the store and buy ice skates. Go home and write a letter to the Ice Capades and ask them to give you a job.

If we had skates, we'd play hockey. We'd have sticks to attack with. We'd have a puck to be concerned with. We would have a purpose.

Basic is a purpose, she says. Did we recall what she had shown us before when she was up in the air on the piano, when she flapped her wings on the plank when we tried to drown her? Did we get it, when she was telling us what it looked like to her, when someone is bound to the earth, and everyone else is *in the air?*

We remember how she had explained this, but spinning and gliding are in waltzes. Waltzes are *slow.* Since when is there jumping in waltzes? Since now, she says.

We make a decision. We'll go along with her. Mrs. Kamsky, we'll go along with you.

We'll go out there and waltz and after we get it going we'll get up there and grab at some air, and she says, if you want to be grabbing at things like a baby, this is what I'll be doing. I'll be closing my eyes, and Davey says, yeah, yeah, let's get up there! Grab some air!

Okay, we won't be babies.

She nods to us. We bow back to her. She plays some more notes of a waltz but we just stand there. For a waltz, you need partners.

Which ones are the partners, and Davey says, not me, I'm the metalworker.

Do we have to pretend that half of the partners are girls?

Davey says, yeah, you do.

She is patient somehow with Davey. Davey, dear, sit down on the floor and be quiet.

It doesn't matter about partners. We should simply just come out by ourselves and hold out our arms and get the feeling that someone is with us, the same as always.

She shows us what to do. She holds out her arms again, one a little higher than the other. In the air like this, her hands are as still as the hands of a statue.

This is how it looks to hold a partner in dancing who isn't there, who is the same to your arms as a thin cloud of air in the shape of a person.

Oh, Lisette, we're saying, and that's how we'll come out, like Lisette had finished dancing just before us.

We show her how we'll do this. It's a start, she says, but now you must think about fire.

She wants to tell us a few things about fire. When I was a child, my home was near a railroad station.

She tells us, even though the station itself was boarded up, and no trains had gone by for many years, and the tracks were broken and rusted, she would look out her window at the glows of fires. There were always old derelict men out there in the cold, lighting fires in rusted barrels. They would burn sticks; bits of litter. If a nearby building was abandoned and falling apart they would fetch a few planks, a part of a wall, and have a much nicer fire with wood.

Wood! says Davey.

This is how we will see it, to begin with, she says. I can see it in my mind how those old men warmed their hands above the barrels.

She looks at us. What's the matter, don't you like it like this?

It's hard for us to picture you in a house like a normal person, growing up.

Well, I was, and I did, same as anyone else.

We would like to know more about your life, but she says, everything I am, is what you are looking at.

Davey's looking in the mirror. He says, I'm not going out there and playing this like I'm homeless, in baggy old pants or something.

Oh, all we have so far is a barrel, she says, and perhaps there are flames. Perhaps today there was a plank from a wall and they have flames coming up above the rim. Perhaps there are worn-down bits of the barrel where we can see the flames inside, as though we're looking into a furnace.

Can we wear tuxedos for the waltz part?

No, we can't, there's no money for costumes. This is for tights.

How about half?

Margaret had just started looking at us from the kitchen doorway. She yells over to us, what half?

The jackets, the neckties, the cool satin thing around the belly. On the bottom, black tights.

That would look pretty good! yells Margaret.

Margaret, says Mrs. Kamsky. Please don't help us.

You need me even if you hate to admit it! yells Margaret.

Then we hear her in the kitchen, banging some things around.

Davey's starting to make some moves. He looks too happy.

She says, no, no, no, no, no, no, no. You are alone, you have no friends. You must be showing us now how you felt about it when your girlfriend turned her back on you and broke your heart, and he stops dead, he freezes for a minute.

He says, I told you that in private.

She waves one hand in a quick small chop at the air. For dancers there is no private. I am speaking of the metalworker, she says.

He starts again. He's got this invisible pair of tongs, which looks like, he says, a sort of tool you'd poke into a furnace.

He's got a hammer, too, and the scissors you use for snipping tin. These invisible things he has to carry, they might be hanging off his belt when he first comes out and we see him.

I've got this big tool belt or something, says Davey.

Ah, the tools in the belt might be heavily weighing him down, she says.

Davey, that's too heavy, do it lighter, lighten up.

She says, wear your belt like the belt of Orion.

Davey's like, oh, sure, no problem. Who's Orion?

A famous giant, says Mrs. Kamsky. In the stars.

I'm a star, he says, and she tells him, not so fast. I am speaking of the sky, the real sky.

We look around at the walls and the mirrors and the air and we say to each other, oh, right, the sky.

She says, you have seen I'm very sure the famous *Wizard of Oz*. The Tin Man, you know, was modeled on the shape of this giant man of stars I am telling you about, in the actual sky.

Tin, says Davey. I'm okay with that, just don't be telling me you want me to look like Dorothy or something.

He goes out and comes in again and looks ten times worse than before.

Is there a mule in *The Wizard of Oz?* No, there's not, so how come Davey looks like some mule, with a great big pack on his back?

It's not a pack, it's a belt, says Davey. I'm supposed to be bummed out.

For this kind of bummed out as you put it we would rush to the drugstore for little white antidepressants, not sit still to watch you dance, she says.

But everything has to stop for a minute because Margaret comes back in. No one around here knows anything about being a mule, except me, she says. What's going on in here?

All of us and Mrs. Kamsky tell her, nothing's going on, we're just having our class, same as always.

I'm sick of just hearing the same thing over and over, but if anything interesting starts happening, like when you really get going on the waltz, someone come and get me, I'll be out in the parlor.

She goes away again and Davey says, I'll lighten up, I don't want to go out there and look like Margaret.

She's mad because we didn't put her in, says Mrs. Kamsky. She thinks the metalworker should have a terrible accident and then a nursemaid can fly from the clouds and fix him up.

I'll be careful, says Davey. He goes out and comes in a little lighter and she starts to play again, but now, for him, she's got it flatter, like a tune for two feet that have not earned the right to leave the ground: dum dum dum dum dum, dum dum, dum dum.

Okay, says Davey, and he's doing some steps. He's by himself in the center, going, I'm like, I'm this metalworker, and I'm the first one there ever was, I'm this prototype tinsmith or something, and no one is around, and I'm all by myself out here, and I'm like really, incredibly bumming.

Mrs. Kamsky starts to play lighter, faster. She looks at us. Was what she taught us all along just something to throw into a hole?

We know what to do. We're ready.

We say to him, Tinsmith, we understand your feelings, even though, at this moment, we don't care about your feelings at all. So just stand there.

We were here first, we say. No one wants to look at you right now. We've been here a long time. We are dancers. We were here before the dinosaurs. You are going to need a spark to start up that barrel, Tinsmith, so, stand still for a couple of minutes and watch us.

This is about something from a long time ago. Books of matches have not yet been invented, we go. If you want to start a fire, you need us.

We say, stand still and be quiet, Tinsmith, and show some respect for the way that we are bringing you fire.

So, we go through it like this, and Margaret comes all the way in again and goes over near the piano and watches us from there.

She says, I think you should let me telephone Lisette, Irene, and tell her that you'll be making the little waltz at the beginning a little longer.

And we go, yeah, call her up.

And Davey's like, he's hitting himself on the head. He says, he can't believe that we're up in the air all over the place and he's working a job that you have to stay earthbound for.

He says, Mrs. Kamsky, before they come out with the fire, can I come out with a couple of jumps? This was supposed to be just my dance.

Oh, we don't need anything jumping around in a scene with a metalworker, she tells him, except the fire.

But it needs to be realistic, says Margaret. It needs to look like a machine shop.

All he has is a little hut, to live in, and he can work in the open, says Mrs. Kamsky.

Like a *shepherd?* says Margaret.

Davey says, I'm not going out there and playing this like Heidi.

He is a metalworker from long ago, with a hut, says Mrs. Kamsky.

Well, don't make the roof with hay or something that'll burn, says Davey.

It's metal, he made it himself, she says, and we picture a hut on a hill or something.

So there's a hut, far away from towns and villages. There's some woods behind it. There's a barrel-like furnace in the yard, this barrel, very old. It's rusty in a couple of places.

We look at these things the way that, if we were going on a trip, we'd take out a map. The hut and the barrel are things on the map we put an x on, to show us the spot where we will land. It's a grim-looking hut, it's a dump, and there's no plumbing. The guy who lives in the hut is *dull*.

Davey says, it could rain. You can't put it out in the open. I can't be out there forging metal and stuff if it's raining, and we're like, the weather's great.

Margaret says, you should put in some drums and have a really bad thunderstorm. He should get struck by the light-ning.

The lightning is for starting the fire, says Mrs. Kamsky.

The nursemaid could fly in on a broomstick. You could attach it on ropes from the ceiling. That would make it really interesting.

Margaret, there's no nursemaid, says Mrs. Kamsky, and we say, there can be a nursemaid in the next one.

You have to have the metalworker making something because that's what metalworkers do, says Margaret, and we're like, it's not that realistic of a dance, and Davey says, it's prototypical.

Margaret says, he shouldn't be wasting his time. He should be making something.

Davey says, I'll make a bunch of screws or nails or something.

Perhaps they would not be screws, they would not be nails, says Mrs. Kamsky. Perhaps they are needles and pins.

If they are, I would have to have some lighter tools, says Davey.

Oh, this is what I'm trying to explain to you, says Mrs. Kamsky.

I never get my way in anything, says Margaret. When are you starting the new dance with the nursemaid?

Soon! we say.

Davey stands there. He'll have some lighter tools, but he thinks more time should go by before we come out, when he's out there near the barrel by himself, and Mrs. Kamsky says to Margaret, I wonder if you wouldn't mind writing it down somewhere that we will give the metalworker another couple of minutes by himself, and Margaret says, I'm not your secretary.

I'll remember it myself, says Davey. I'll come out before the lightning and go through the positions or something by myself, real basic, don't worry about it, and then I'll do a few jumps.

You're *grounded,* Davey, we say, and Margaret says, to help us out, the Tin Man's too heavy to be jumping. He has to stay put on the ground. Isn't this what you were saying before?

Davey says, I'm the least heaviest kid in here, if you don't count the monkey, and Margaret looks around in case the monkey is under the piano again or hanging off the barre. But she's home, doing her homework.

Mrs. Kamsky says to Davey, the tinsmith is heavy from sad, not heavy from his body.

He's lonesome, he's way bummed out, says Davey.

But he is someone who is going to be lucky, someone who is being delivered some fire, she tells him.

It gets quiet. She looks at us and there is a strange look on her face. We've never seen her look like this before. We would like to know what she is thinking. But we know what will happen if we ask such a basic question. She'll say, go home.

She says, I wonder if perhaps you might consider, the next time you come, that you have come here to light a fire in a barrel, not to burn down the world, and Davey says, let up on the bolts, you guys.

She says, as you are dancing a waltz while you are bringing us fire, I would like to suggest to you that simply having one bolt would be sufficient.

She says, I will see you tomorrow. Anyone can start a little fire one time. We will see what's going on with this fire of yours when you come back tomorrow, that is, if you happen to remember tomorrow what you did.

She bends over the piano and starts playing again, and it's the same music we just got done dancing to, so, even if she's sitting there playing it for just herself and Margaret, we listen to it while we're putting our clothes back on.

Margaret says, I'm not waiting till dark to call up Lisette when the rates go down, Irene.

Please don't talk to me when I'm playing the piano like this, and Margaret says, oh, sorry.

We put on our clothes on top of our tights.

We just take off our clothes when we come in and kick them away in some corner and then it takes us a long time to get everything sorted out, because it's not like there're showers and locker rooms around here.

We take a long time getting dressed. It takes us fifteen minutes to tie our shoelaces.

We keep listening to what she's playing. Dah dah dah dah dah, dah dah, dah dah, dah dah dah dah dah, dah dah, dah dah, just a basic old start of a waltz.

She goes light on the keys for when we head toward the x of the hut and it's like we're listening to a music box. She leans into it. It's like we're feeling the notes in the belly.

When she goes faster, it's like beating at the air. When she goes slower, it's like we can feel what it's like to have a little longer space between one beat of your heart and then the next one.

We listen to her. This is different playing from other times. The notes of the music are going into us in the part of the brain where we know basic things, such as, food goes into your mouth, sleeping takes place in the nighttime, the sun comes up every day.

Slow, fast, heavy, light, fast, heavy, light, slow. We're storing it up, so that, when we leave her today and go home, we still hear it.

Heavy, light, fast, heavy. Light, slow, slow, fast. Heavy, light. Fast, heavy. Light, slow, slow, fast, heavy, light, light, light, light, light, light.

The whole time, inside our heads, until we're here with her tomorrow, we still can hear what she played for us, and all along, when we're walking around in the world, even if we look like normal people, we're still dancing.

the silver monkey

FIRST, I COME OUT and show the people who I am. Some music starts playing.

I have to make the people think that, as soon as they see me come out, they are glad that they can see me. I must come out very lightly. I must walk with my head held up high. I must not look up directly into the lights. I must not be afraid of how bright they are.

The people just paid a lot of money for their ticket. When I come out and they see me, they must not get nervous about that. They must not start thinking to themselves, oh, no, was the money for my ticket like money poured into a hole?

But when I first come out, I do not have to make them believe right away that this is worth it. I only have to make them glad that they can see me.

They will want to feel hope. But they will not want to have it happen that all of their hope comes out at once. They could enjoy it very much if they can feel a little nervousness about whether or not I'll let them down, when they went to so much trouble to come and see me.

They will sit and be quiet. No one can be moving around on their feet but the ballerina. No one else can stand up except the conductor, and no one can be lit up in lights except the ballerina. If some ushers stand up near the doors when the ballerina comes out, then, someone must tell them to sit down.

When I first come out I do not have to have my eyes all the way open. I can have both my eyes a little closed.

I must start to see the lights very slowly. I must let my eyes get used to them.

When I open my eyes all the way, I will see that the lights are the lights of the stars, and everyone is sleeping in their beds, except the little silver monkey.

This is the time when the little silver monkey comes out. She comes out to dance in her neighborhood. She holds her head back. She stands up on her toes. She jumps and twirls and spins. She knows that the stars are far away. But she is going to talk to them anyway.

This is what she does. She comes out and talks to the stars. She comes out and has a talk with the sky. She lets the people come and watch her. She will think of the things that people in the seats would want to say to the stars and the sky, if the people in the seats knew how to do this. She will try to say those things for the people.

This is what I will do.

First, I will speak for myself to tell the people who I am, and then I will speak for the people. Then, I will try to tell the people what the sky and the stars were saying back.

I do not want people in the seats to look at their watches in the shadows and wish that intermission would hurry.

I do not want the people in the seats to go away and not remember me. I do not want the people to go to bed and then wake up the next morning without making it happen that, the first thing they see, in the backs of their eyes, before they lift up their head from the pillow, is what I had looked like the night before when I was dancing, and they had seen me. "There's the silver monkey, at the backs of my eyes," they must say. They would not have to say to themselves, "Oh, I wish I was sleeping and dreaming, which is nicer than actual life." They could see me whenever they wanted to in their memory, when they're awake. When the memory starts to wear off, then, they can come back and see me again.

If I start to feel afraid about these things when I come out, I must not be afraid of the people. I must say to myself, "My feet will remember the steps."

I must not scamper off into the trees.

Perhaps I should say to myself, oh, look how quiet it is, perhaps all the people have gone to sleep. Perhaps when I speak to the people, they will think that I am speaking to them in their dreams. Perhaps, when I am dancing, they are part of the show.

They are all the sleeping people in the neighborhood. Only the silver monkey can stay up late.

If I am frightened of the lights, after I've come out, I must start to do the steps a little earlier than how we planned it. This would be okay with the piano. The piano would be used to this kind of thing.

When I am dancing the steps, I will see that, they are something to really be glad for. As long as there are steps for me to do, I will not feel so very afraid.

I must say to myself, oh, I know who I am when I am dancing. I am a little silver monkey, I must say.

This is the kind of dancer I must be. I must never be pretty like Sleeping Beauty and Cinderella, who have oatmeal and empty air inside their heads instead of a brain. Sleeping Beauty and Cinderella did not know a way to come out in the night all alone and be able to speak, as I will. And you will not have to wonder what it is that I am saying when I talk this way. You will only have to look at me, and you will know.

This is how it is for me when I dance. It must always be the same thing that I am thinking.

I must remember that, when I open my eyes all the way, I must never imagine that the lights are like the sun. I must always imagine that, when I am dancing, it is always, always night.

Perhaps later on when I have learned a lot more, I will not
be able to bear what this is like. Or perhaps I will be able to
bear it. No one knows what will come. We'll have to see.

I should not be afraid. I must step into the air very lightly,
and raise my arms out, oh, very slowly. I must hold my mouth
closed so that my lips are always together, except for a little
tiny bit.

I must never let the piano speak for me. I must speak in
the steps, with my arms and my head and my feet.

I will not be able to see the people in the seats. But I must
make them sit up straighter. When their eyes have to blink, it
must seem to them that, the smallest of blinks is too long.
They will want to only look at me as a clever and funny little monkey.

But this is what will happen instead. When I am doing the
steps, their hope will rise up inside them. It will rise like a
flame of a match. I will see what this is like. I will feel what
this is like with all my skin.

This is what I will do. First, I will come out in this manner and let you see me, and then I'll go up on my toes. I will
hold out my arms a certain way.

I will turn very slowly, and face the sky. Now, when I
do this, I am not just a small little monkey any longer. This
is my job.

You will look at me again. I will see that it is always the
same. When I open up my eyes a little wider, so will you.

Now the music will play, and I will come out and let you
see me. Then I will turn, and I will look far away from you,
way over your heads, toward the cold and beautiful stars, and
start speaking.